FRIEND ZONED

BY,

WREN MICHAELS

A

Editor: Margaret Bail

Formatting: eBook Builders

Cover Art: LeTeisha Newton with Boundless Tales Designs

All's fair in love and war until one person gets stuck in an arranged marriage.

Catherine 'Cat' Marek has a sociology paper due on dissecting the laws of attraction. Project Panty Drop will case study two different men; one she'll go after in person and the other she'll attempt to charm online. Hiding behind her beauty, she tries to cover up her true geeky side, and the fact that she's partially deaf.

Jaidev 'Jai' Sankar needs to knock out a paper for his online sociology class. After an encounter with the Texas Tease, Cat Marek, he decides Project Friend Zoned will be the ultimate topic, proving a guy can remain in the friend zone with a girl he finds attractive.

As Cat puts the moves into overdrive, Jai finds it harder to remain in the 'friend zone' with her. The only thing keeping him from letting go is the fact his hardcore Hindu parents have a wedding scheduled for him. When neither can resist their attraction, the fight no longer becomes about their papers, but about the freedom to love each other.

CONTENTS

ACKNOWLEDGMENTS:

So many people to say thanks to for helping me with this book. First and foremost, my Crit Partners who believed in this book from its onset: Jennifer, Sonia, Kristy, Evie, and LeTeisha. Thanks for your insight, support, and cheers. Second, to my agent, Margaret, for championing this book with me and taking the time to make it the best it could be. Third, to LeTeisha for all her hard work helping me come up with a cover that would really convey the depth of the book. Next to Deena and my Badass Book Bitches who have encouraged me and supported me on this new path, thank you from the bottom of my heart. And last, all my love to my husband who has supported me from the get go about my writing career. I love you!!

DEDICATION:

To those who have to fight for love, in a world where it's taken for granted.

CHAPTER 1

CAT

Beer dribbled down my chin as a breath hitched in my throat mid-drink. A line of suds trailed from my neck into the vast crevice of my breasts, never to be seen again. I muffled a cough as my eyes followed God's gift to lady bits toward the bar. Sleeves rolled to the elbows, his white button-down shirt contrasted his olive skin. From the mess of tousled dark-brown hair, I figured he'd probably come to quench his thirst after a nooner. Lucky bitch.

The Longhorn game ruined my view, as a sea of students swarmed a giant flat-screen on the wall and swallowed his body. Normally, I'd be up there cheering right along with them, but Angie hated football. So like a good BFF, I hung at the booth with her.

"It's so loud in here I can't hear myself think. You're lucky." Angie quirked a brow and handed me a napkin. "You okay, Cat?"

Yup, lucky me. I gave her a nod. "Fine."

I let my gaze fall away from reading her lips down to my hand patting its way into my bra as discreetly as possible.

"Uh huh. Which one is he?" she asked, not trying very hard to hide her sly grin.

As my roommate for the last several years, it was hard to

hide anything from her. I leaned in. "The one in the white oxford."

She jerked back. "The Bollywood model?"

"Shh," I hissed through clenched teeth, shooting her a wide-eyed glare.

"Oh yeah, he's yum. Seen him a few times on campus. No idea what his name is though. You want me to find out?" She inched her way to the edge of the booth.

"No!" I clasped a hand on her arm. "Chill, Ang."

Dipping her chin, she locked eyes with me. "Chicken-shit."

I gave her my finest death stare. "I've got a plan. I can kill two birds with one stone."

"I like plans. Are we gonna tag team? From the looks of those muscles, he could probably bench press both of us."

I inched my way across the table, closing the distance between us. "Back off, sister. I saw him first."

"You're lucky I *love* you like a sister." She sat back in the booth. "Lay your plan on me."

"I think I just found the first target for my sociology term paper." I glanced over my shoulder to the bar. Mr. Bollywood fist pumped a Longhorn tackle and took a chug of dark beer.

"Okay, deets." She sipped her white wine and bounced a leg under the table.

I spun back around and sifted through the noise around me for discernible words. "Huh?"

"Details. Spill it." Angie set her glass back down, flagging the waitress for another.

"Oh, I'm dissecting the laws of attraction. In today's social media age full of chatrooms, dating sites, and selfies, I thought it would be interesting to compare the old-fashioned way of meeting a guy in person versus getting to know someone online."

"Interesting, go on," Angie said.

"I'll pick two targets. One guy I'm going to throw myself at in person, really working up the tangible side of things from simple physical attraction to touch and feel. The other I'm going to approach online, using words, wit, and charm." I slipped a notepad from my book bag and jotted down some notes before I forgot anything. "I'll see which one tries to get me in bed first."

"Smooth. Get laid and a term paper done. Well played,

Catherine Marek. Well played." Her blue eyes twinkled in the beam of sunlight filtering between the slats of the blinds. "I totally should've come up with that one myself."

"I'm not doing it to get laid." I shook my head. "I'm trying to prove a point. If you flash tits, they'll drop 'trou'. I don't expect it to last more than a couple of hours before I'm calling a cab." I sat back and folded my arms. "Online, you get to know a person. Inside-out first."

She arched a brow. "Mm-hmm, well, just make sure the objects of your mission aren't in Sociology with you."

"Well, Mr. Bollywood over there isn't. I sure as hell would've noticed him. We've been in class for a month, and I've never seen him." I took a swig of my beer, managing to keep it in my mouth this time.

Angie picked at her damp napkin as she glanced around the dimly lit bar. "So, he's gonna be your in-person target?"

I traced the outline of a condensation droplet streaking my pint glass. "So far, he's looking like a good pick. He's brawny, into sports, and likes beer. Almost stereotypical college guy. I'm thinking he'll probably respond if I target him with outright flirting. Can't set myself up for failure, ya know?" Switching into stealth mode, I did my best to toss a side glance in his direction. He caught me as he turned from the bar and made his way to a nearby table, sitting across from a sandy-blond guy that may have been in my Economics class.

Rich, espresso-colored eyes locked onto mine for a brief second and a flutter ransacked my heart, sending it dive-bombing straight to my stomach. He glanced away as quick as I did.

"I think he just looked at you," Angie said.

I stared into the amber liquid in front of me, studying the tiny carbonated bubbles zipping to the top. With each breath I sucked into my lungs, my heart hammered a little faster.

"Cat," Angie said.

I shook my head. "Huh?"

"I said, he looked right at you." Angie nodded her head to the left with wide eyes.

"I know." I gripped the edge of the table, forcing down my speeding heart. Something about his eyes hit me harder than expected. Maybe I needed to find a different target.

She gave my arm a nudge. "Well, no time like the present. Go flirt and find out his name."

"Nope, gotta find my other target first. I have to start them at the same time to make sure the playing field is level. But now I know he comes in here, so I'll just have to frequent the pub a little more often. And, I have to make sure he's single." I swallowed hard over the air wedged in my throat.

"True, would definitely tank your results if he's already banging someone." Angie nodded. "As hot as he is, I'm guessing his peen is seeing some action."

I glanced in his direction one more time, catching a gorgeous smile spreading over his lips as he laughed at something his friend said. "Well, let's test it. I'll head to the ladies room. You watch him and see if he notices me. If he's in a solid relationship, chances are he'll pay no attention and be focused on the game and his friend."

"Cat, the man has a penis. You're gorgeous, petite, and have tits. Doesn't matter if he's in a solid relationship, he'll pay attention to you." She pursed her lips.

I narrowed my eyes. "Just humor me. Let's see if he has any interest."

"Okay. I'm in watch mode. Go for it." She leaned against the table, and long locks of ash-blonde hair fell over her shoulders.

I glanced down, making sure nothing had stained my white blouse in the drinking debacle from earlier. The girls sat perky in their place with no beer blemish in sight thanks to the top two buttons left open. Sliding from the booth proved to be a less than graceful exit. The back of my thighs stuck to the pleather seats due to the four hundred and ninety percent humidity in Texas. I pressed my hands the length of the black skirt, and the fabric brushed the back of my thigh, confirming it wasn't tucked into some weird place.

Guys dug the school-girl look, and I said a silent thank you to Angie for advising me to wear it to the bar this afternoon. Putting a little extra sway in my hips, I took a slow stroll past Mr. Bollywood's table on my way to the restroom. I fought the urge to give him a glance along the way and almost won out. As I passed his table, I gave a quick look over my shoulder, letting my fingertips graze the thick lacquer coating on the wood-paneled walls.

We locked eyes again. My heart stopped, and I forced back a gasp. A peanut rolled under my shoe, and my ankle wobbled as it crunched beneath my heel. I nearly knocked over a server doing a perfect pirouette out of my way as I hit the bathroom door. Thankfully, we both stuck the landing. Once inside, I leaned against the wall and let out the gasp in a slow, methodical breath.

"Holy shit," I mumbled.

"You all right there?" a girl asked, reaching for a towel from the dispenser on the wall next to me.

Startled, I shook my head and gave her a smile. "Yeah, I'm good, thanks."

I plunked myself into one of the stalls and summoned the strength for the walk back. Holy hell he was hot. I'd never had any trouble getting a guy to notice me. Not that I was drop dead gorgeous, or even remotely sexy. But I'd classify myself as cute, and managed to turn a head or two. Something I relied on to compensate for my natural affliction toward geekiness, and the fact that I was deaf.

This little experiment may tank if I couldn't get my shit together. Maybe I needed to find a different target. One not so good looking.

I had no intention of sleeping with either of the targets. I'd explain things to them after the ruse was up and thank them for their time with my term paper. But on the other hand, if I *could* get that one into bed with me? Bonus points. I'd dated around in my time at UT Austin, but I'd never encountered one that made my head spin and heart hammer just from a look.

I glanced at my watch. Crap! I'd been in the bathroom for nearly ten minutes. The dude would probably think I took a dump. I face-palmed myself and made my way to the sink to wash up. After making sure my eyeliner hadn't melted off my face and putting on a fresh coat of lipstick, I sucked in a deep breath and headed back to my booth.

My heart sank as I eyed their empty table on my way back. I scanned the bar, even did a twirl looking around the room for the mysterious man, with no luck. The only remnants of them was the scent of stale beer and orgasm-inducing cologne.

I let a pout ride my lips as I made my way to the booth.

Angie's wry grin softened as I climbed in. "Yeah, he took off right after you nearly took out the waitress. Which is good 'cause what the hell were you doing in there, taking a dump?"

"Sorry, was distracted. So did he look?" My voice notched an octave higher than I'd intended.

"Of course. Just like I said. And you very well know he looked, cause you looked right back at him, Ms. Not-so-stealthy." She folded her arms.

"I wonder why he left? The game's still on, and the bar's full." I glanced around hoping I'd maybe missed him in the sea of people.

She shrugged. "Dunno. Probably had a date."

"You're not helping." I glared at her.

"Just being realistic. The guy's built like Adonis. There's no way he's not poking his penis into something. He's probably gay. He dresses too nice for your typical college guy. Half the dudes in my classes are in sweats." Angie took a long swill of her wine, finishing it off.

"True. But maybe he's metrosexual. You know, gets like manicures and pedicures to look good for the ladies. I'm okay with some manscaping." I downed the last of my beer, then let out a defeated sigh.

She chucked a couple bucks on the table and slung her purse over her shoulder. "I think you need to find a different guy. Come with me to a house party tonight. You can find another hottie there to take his place."

I added some cash to hers and scooted out of the booth. "Maybe. Doesn't hurt to keep my options open. I haven't solidified my choice on the online target yet."

She lowered her head and dug out her keys from the depths of her purse. "Good. Wanna come shopping with me? Need to find an outfit for tonight."

"Huh?" I shielded my eyes from the bright sunshine as we exited the dark bar. "You turned away from me."

"Oh, sorry." Angie's apologetic smile appeared as she raised her head, looking at me face to face. "Want to hit the mall with me?"

"Naw, I'm gonna head back to the dorm and see if I can find my online target at least. When's the shindig tonight?"

"Eight. It's at a house just off campus."

"Okay, I'll meet you back at the room." I leaned in and gave her a brisk hug.

I made the jaunt from the bar back to the dorms quicker than I thought. Possibly because thoughts of Mr. Bollywood inundated me and I lost all concept of time. Those dark-brown bedroom eyes nearly swallowed me from across the room. Full, luscious lips hid behind dark stubble. I imagined the whiskers scratching my skin as we kissed, and I tripped over the threshold into my dorm room. I prayed no one witnessed it.

Shaking it off, I chucked my book bag onto my bunk and sat at my desk. I flipped through page after page of online personals in the Austin area; nothing seemed to really catch my eye. A few possibilities made it to my maybe pile, but location tossed them back out the window. I needed someone near campus, not on far ends of the city. I banged my head on my folded arms on the desk. Here I thought it'd be easy to just find someone online and flirt with them.

Online conversations were a lot less stressful. I never had to ask people to repeat themselves, never missed words, or had to struggle to filter the noise my hearing aids picked up. I could just be me without worry. My messenger alert dinged, and my head shot up off the desk. One new private message. A smile curled over my lips when I saw the screen name *WhoDat*.

My smile got even bigger. I don't know why it didn't occur to me earlier. He just became my other target.

I'd talked to *WhoDat* off and on for the last couple months, meeting in a chatroom discussing one of our favorite TV shows, Doctor Who. At one time he said he was from New Orleans, or he liked the New Orleans Saints, but moved to Austin recently. I couldn't really remember. But so far, he hadn't shown any tendencies toward the criminally insane. He would probably be safe enough to eventually meet up with.

While technically I already knew the guy, I'd never remotely flirted with him, or gave any indication I wanted anything more than to discuss wibbly wobbly timey wimey stuff with him. Moving him up into the category of target would still be level playing ground compared to the in-person target. And it's not like we had some solid ongoing friendship I'd destroy if things went south after the big reveal on Project Panty Drop.

I went to work, putting the wheels in motion.

Step One—The Flirt Zone.

WhoDat: Hey, Impossible Girl.

Me: Well, 'ello!

WhoDat: Ready to watch the new episode tonight?

Me: I can't. I promised my roomie I'd go to this stupid party with her tonight. I'll have to watch it tomorrow.

WhoDat: Yeah, I got suckered into plans tonight, too. So I watched the BBC viewing online. :)

Me: No Way! Cheater. You're naughty.

WhoDat: Why yes, yes I am. Naughty that is, not a cheater. ;)

Me: No Spoilers.

WhoDat: You sure? It's really good ...

Me: No. Yes. No. Maybe. Ugh, why must you torture me?

WhoDat: Because I know you like it.

Me: I do, do I?

WhoDat: Hey, just cuz we're online doesn't mean you can't get to know a person.

Me: True dat.

WhoDat: Oy! Don't be stealin' my lines now, Impossible Girl. ;)

Me: Listen Sweetie, don't be mixin'

Doctors and Companions. ;)

WhoDat: I'd much rather be mixing drinks and watching the episode in tandem with you.

Me: Me too. I'm not really looking forward to this party.

WhoDat: Why not?

Me: I don't like large crowds and noise. Plus, I'll probably just say stupid Firefly and Doctor Who references to people who will have no idea what I'm talking about. I'm a great facilitator of awkward silence.

WhoDat: Won't your boyfriend swoop in and protect you?

Me: If I had one, maybe. But then again he'd probably be as geeky as me, and we'd both be standing there like awkward turtles. LOL

WhoDat: Or, you'd be at home with him watching Who and not even go to the lame-ass party.

Me: Correct! But alas, I made a promise to my BFF to go, so I suppose I should get ready.

WhoDat: Well, I shall wait to torture you more tomorrow then. I've gotta run myself right now. Just saw you online and wanted to say hi. Have a fun time at your party.

Me: You too. Night!

A smile curled my lips, and a little twinge of happiness zinged my heart. This may actually turn out to be fun. Glancing at my alarm clock, I had thirty minutes to get ready for the party, and hopefully my other target.

CHAPTER 2

JAI

Her face haunted me. The adorable dimple pitted in her cheek caught my eye first. Sexy full lips that folded into a gorgeous smile just about took my breath away. I did my best not to continuously stare at her, managing to throw just a few glances here and there hoping she got the message. But she didn't take the bait. Instead, she gave me a 'too good for you' glance while she plowed down a server on her way to the bathroom, probably to restock the toilet paper in her bra.

The Texas Tease, I called it. Lots of girls at UT had it—this one in particular—in spades. Shorter than my normal tastes, her alluring doe-eyes caught me off guard. The memory of her petite frame sashaying as she worked those sexy, black pumps played on a loop in my head. Along with the way her long, brown hair bounced with every step like a damn shampoo commercial.

She drove me insane, and I didn't even know her name. At least Mick confirmed she was a student at UT, apparently in one of his Economics classes.

She intrigued me, sitting in a sports bar drinking beer while her prissy friend sipped wine. I even caught her glancing at the Longhorn game on the big screen. A cute girl who likes beer and football? Every guy's dream. If only she weren't a snob. But, I'd put her in her place. And I had the perfect plan.

The ring of my Skype alert disrupted my plotting. Incoming message from Kanti, my best friend.

Kanti: Hey ...

Me: What's up, brat?

Kanti: You busy?

Me: Never too busy for you.

Kanti: Stop with the sugar, you're giving me diabetes.

Me: LOL Better get used to it.

Kanti: Ugh. Don't remind me. Quick, what do you want for your birthday? You got the new Mortal Kombat release already?

Me: Yeah, of course I do. But you don't have to get me anything. You know that.

Kanti: I can't NOT get you anything.

Me: Tell me you talked to your parents and the wedding's called off. That would be an awesome present.

Kanti: Seriously? You know that isn't even in the realm of possibilities. So shut it.

Me: I can dream, can't I?

Kanti: Yeah, and I know what you do in those dreams. Not even going there.

Me: You're such a bitch. Why do I love you?

Kanti: Because we're best friends.

Me: Well, there's that.

Mick yelled through the door. "Jai, you comin' down or what?"

"In a minute," I replied.

Me: I gotta go. Kegger tonight and we're hosting.

Kanti: Email me and let me know what to get you.

Me: Fine.

Kanti: LOL Kiss Kiss

Me: Whatever. LOL TTYL

I closed the lid on my laptop as Mick flung the door open. "People are starting to arrive. You're on keg duty first."

I tossed him a nod. "Yeah, I know. I'm coming. Just finishing up some notes on my Sociology project."

"I thought you dropped that class?" He folded his arms, leaning against the door-frame.

"I was going to until Professor Wilkinson agreed to let me take it online, since it's the same time as my cinematography course." I pulled out a notepad. "What'd you say that chick's name was again? The one we saw at the bar today."

"Catherine Marek. But I think she goes by Cat." Mick shrugged. "Why? I thought you said she was a snob, and you weren't gonna pursue her?"

"Oh, I'm not. I got my sights set on another girl I've been talking to for a little while. But I think that Cat chick will make for a perfect target on my sociology paper." I wrote down her name and underlined it five times. "I'm calling it, Friend Zoned."

Mick laughed. "Oh, this ought to be good. What're you gonna do?"

"It's what I'm not gonna do that's going be the best part. I'm going to act like I'm interested, then when she takes the bait, I'll friend zone her. I'm going to prove that a guy can be sexually attracted to a girl who's interested in him and still remain only friends. I'll be the best 'friend' she's ever gonna have."

"So, if she dissed you at the bar, how do you expect to get her to go after you?" Mick narrowed his eyes.

"I'll come to her rescue." I grinned.

Mick raised a brow. "How do you plan on doing that?"

"I'll have one of the other guys hit on her big time. Then I'll dive in and save her from his claws. She'll be thankful, thinking the gesture romantic and open up to me." I placed a hand over my heart. "Plant the seed, Mick. Plant the seed. Chicks dig it when you swoop in and save them from the big bad wolf." I slid my notebook under my laptop and made my way to the door.

"Dude, she's gonna blow your house down." Mick laughed with a shake of his head.

I narrowed my eyes. "Care to place a wager?"

"You're on. Hundred bucks says she blows you off."

"Better call your dad for a loan." I nudged his shoulder as I passed him in the hallway.

"Whatever, dick. Might as well pay up now," Mick said, chasing after me.

Loud music filled the house, the thumping bass rattling the windows. I made my way to the back yard to the keg on the lawn. A sea of people swarmed every room as I worked back and forth filling red solo cups and delivering them to the awaiting masses.

A leggy blonde set her sights on me. The heat from her already drunk eyes welled up on my neck, right before the vomit inducing alcohol breath hit my nose.

"Hi, Jaheedeeev," she said, in more of a hiccup than a word.

She tripped into my arms, and I caught her before she went down. But not before she sloshed her drink all over my white shirt.

"It's Jaidev, like Chai Dave. Make it simple, call me Jai, like everyone else." I eased her to a stance, and by sheer luck into a lawn chair.

"Sexy, Jahideev," she slurred and took another drink of beer.

I inched myself away from her, trying to find who she might belong to. Thankfully my parents, who actually owned the house, were in Houston and not here to witness the kegger debacle. They didn't want me wasting my college days living in some frat house full of parties. So they bought a house close to campus and agreed to let me and some of my friends rent it during our college years.

Somehow Mick and the others talked me into a small party tonight. Clearly their definition of small and mine differed.

The beer and smoke smell wafting up from my shirt almost made me gag. I had to get myself a new shirt. I slid it off my shoulders and curled it into a ball, elbowing my way through the growing crowd.

I turned the corner in the living room and smacked right into *her*. That Cat girl. Well, technically she smacked into me. Her face landed against my bare chest, and we bounced off each other. The music disappeared. The people vanished. Everything around me halted. Her soft brown eyes swallowed me whole as they opened wide in surprise.

Perfect, pink pouty lips left their mark on my chest as I glanced at her smudged lipstick and then to the outline of them on my left nipple. Almost like it had been intended. Words failed to make it out of my mouth. My thundering heart made it impossible to think straight. We continued to stare at each other before her friend rudely interrupted our wordless conversation.

"Well, that was awkward," she said, pulling Cat away from me.

"It's … okay," I managed to say, somewhat coherently. This chick blew me away. I feared this Project Friend Zone may end up harder than I thought. "Sorry, I was on a mission to get a clean shirt. Some drunk freshie just tried to drown me in her beer."

"No, it's my fault. Wasn't paying attention. I'm sorry." Cat raised a hand to swipe at the lipstick on my skin, but pulled back. Pink flooded her cheeks, a similar shade to what colored my nipple. It contrasted her beautiful deep-brown eyes.

"Could've been worse." I formed a sly smile, forcing back my own threatening blush.

Her fingertips hovered over my skin, sending heated awareness rampaging through me in the form of goosebumps. I had to get out of there before she got any sense of what her presence did to me. Not to mention I had to regroup and figure out a new plan, since I had no idea she'd show up tonight. I thought I'd have time to try and stage something at the bar in the next week or so.

"Excuse me, I need to head upstairs and grab a clean shirt."

I gave her what I hoped came out to be a sincere smile and took off toward the stairs, doing everything in my power not to look back at her. I wouldn't let her get the best of me.

From the corner of my eye, I glanced her direction as I made my way up the stairs. Her lips remained parted as she followed me with her eyes, surprise still filling them. Interesting. Maybe I'd gotten to her after all. Still, had to solidify the plan. Just because she was gorgeous didn't mean I'd let her out of it.

I made it to my room and slammed the door shut. A whoosh rushed from my lips as I let out the air wedged in my throat. Tossing my ruined shirt in the laundry, I pulled out another from my closet. As I slid the black button-down over my shoulders, the pink on my skin caught my eye. I stared at it in the mirror reliving the instant her soft lips hit my skin, and a burst of heat shot to my dick. Shaking my head, I forced myself to think of anything but her.

Focus on the plan, Jai. Focus.

I gave myself a once over in the mirror. Maybe undo one more button on the shirt, enough for her to see the lipstick still on my chest. A sly grin rolled over my lips as I headed back to the hallway where I spotted one of my friends.

"Yo, Brent!" I called out to the end of the hall.

He spun on his heel and wandered over.

"What's up, Jai?" he asked, holding a cup of brew.

I tossed him a nod. "Need a favor, man."

He made his way over.

"Can you paw at a girl for me so I can swoop in and rescue her from your clutches?" I leaned against the wall and gave him a knowing grin.

"How far you want me to take it? I don't wanna get slapped with a restraining order," he said with a laugh.

"Naw. Just stalk her a bit, then come on to her real hard. I'll keep an eye out and dive in before she thinks you'll cross the line. No worries, man," I reassured him.

"Who's your target?"

"A girl named Catherine Marek. Goes by Cat. You know her?" I asked.

Brent gave a nod. "Yeah, I think we've got an English class

together. Short, hot girl with dark brown hair?"

My fingers dug into my arms when he hit the word hot. True, she was, but the fact he called her so sent a twinge of jealousy through me. It threw me for a loop. I barely knew the girl, and the little I did made me not even like her.

"That's the one. She's downstairs with her friend. So beware, the friend may try and throw you off. I'll do my best to get there before she does."

"Okay. You ready, cause I don't want Lizzy seeing me hit on another chick. We already had a fight once this month, and it took me two weeks to get laid again. You've got twenty minutes before she gets here." Brent took off down the hall.

Regret hit me. I forgot he had a girlfriend. The last thing I wanted was for him to lose his girl as a result of any of this. Brent was an okay dude, but got mighty cranky when he wasn't getting laid on a regular basis. Most of the guys I lived with had either a bed buddy or a steady girlfriend. I'd have asked Mick to do it, but Cat already saw us together at the pub. She'd know something was up if he approached her, and I came out like the hero. It had to be someone she didn't know.

"I'm gonna put a little space between us. You go in and find her, and I'll keep watch." I fought the grin inching its way over my lips. Project Friend Zone was about to take flight.

He turned around and stared me straight in the eyes. "Okay, but if you see Lizzy you get me the hell out of there immediately. Got it?"

"Don't worry. Go, you're wasting time." I ushered him down the hall with a shove.

Hanging at the top of the stairs, I glanced over the crowd in search of her. Brent's six-foot-three height made it easy to track him. I followed his head of blond hair through the mass of people. But he ducked into one of the side rooms, and I lost him. I barreled my way down the stairs to catch up to him.

Crazy drunk girl cut me off mid stride. "Jayeeeee," she slurred. "I found you, you snucky deveeeel."

I mumbled a string of obscenities. "Listen, sweetie, why don't you find yourself a place to sit, and I'll go get us some drinks?"

"Okay." She barely got the word out before the vomit followed. All over my shoe.

I banged my head against the wall next to me. Seriously?

"I'm sowwy, Jayeeeee." Bloodshot eyes stared up at me, leaking water down her cheeks.

Or it could've been beer. Toss up. But a twinge of remorse hit me. As much as I wanted to be a dick and leave her there, I didn't have it in me to let her wallow in her own puke.

I clutched her to my side and worked my way to the downstairs bathroom. As I yanked open the door, a couple making out on the toilet squealed. At least they remained fully clothed.

"Sorry guys. Out." I thumbed over my shoulder. "Need the facilities."

Disgruntled huffs and curses followed them out the door. I worked to clean up Pukey McPukerson and get the remnants of her barf off my shoe as well. Her body slumped over the toilet, and she clutched the Dallas Cowboy Cheerleader shower curtain, burying her face in a pair of perky breasts. Out like a light. Probably wouldn't even remember it in the morning. Unfortunately, I would.

The scent of vomit filled the bathroom, and my own stomach itched to heave. I hadn't even had a beer yet. Slinging her into my arms, I made my way from the bathroom to the living room and kicked off another couple making out on the sofa to lay the girl down.

I glanced at my watch. Five minutes before Lizzy's scheduled appearance. Sniffing the air, the smell of vomit still clung to me. No way could I swoop in and save Cat from Brent smelling like that. In a mad dash, I lunged up the stairs, two at a time, pushing people out of my way.

I tossed my sneakers in the trash and threw on the first thing I grabbed out of my closet—a raggedy old pair of jeans and a Captain America t-shirt. It lacked in sexy, but it hugged my biceps making me look ripped. It would have to do. I didn't even bother with shoes as I tore out of my room and back downstairs in time to catch Lizzy coming in the door with her entourage of gal pals.

Shit. Brent would be a goner if I didn't get there in time. Diving and rolling, I weaved through the mass of people doing my best to try and remember where Pukey had left her mark so I didn't step in it barefoot.

I caught them in one of the back rooms, and he had Cat pinned to the wall. One hand rested above her head as he inched his way into her personal space. Her body slid lower along the wall, clearly trying to wiggle free of his invasion. Mick had her friend occupied across the room. Oh, well done, guys. I owed them a case of beer.

I skidded into the room and brushed Brent right into the wall next to him, and me right up against Cat. Just as Lizzy made her way around the corner.

Cat stared up at me, her stunning brown doe-eyes wide open.

"Hi again," I said between heaving breaths.

"Hi." Her attention drew back to Brent over my shoulder as Lizzy wrapped her arms around him, pulling him into a deep kiss. The smacking of their lips in my ear told me so.

"I hope Brent wasn't being a jackhole." I pulled back from her, realizing our chests pressed against each other again. Her nipples grazed my torso, sending a spine-tingling shiver down my back.

"Were you saving me from him? Or him from the wrath of his girlfriend?" She folded her arms and quirked a brow.

Shit.

"Both." Shoving my hands in my pockets, I managed a smile and took another step back. "Might as well be honest." Well, so much for that plan. I had nothing else left but to play the loyalty card.

"Something to be said for honesty." She eyed me up and down before pointing at my feet. "You seem to have forgotten your shoes in your rush to swoop in and save me."

A laugh popped from my throat. "You have no idea what I've gone through in the last fifteen minutes."

"Do tell. A man who risks a house-party floor without shoes during a kegger says a lot." Her lips curled into a sexy smile as she pushed off the wall and brushed against me.

An erratic thump beat through my heart, and I forced a deep breath. That smile with those eyes, they were like weapons. And she knew how to use them. But I had to keep on mission. I had no time to find another target. Already a month late on it, I had to get my project going or I'd fall behind, and I needed to get it done before leaving for India at winter break.

"I'll spill my secrets over a beer if you'll join me?" I offered her my arm.

She slid hers through the crook of my elbow, and I escorted her to the backyard.

Bait taken. Challenge accepted.

CHAPTER 3

CAT

The pounding bass still pulsated in my veins and thudded in my already sensitive ears. I'd never been so happy to get out of the house. After rounding up a couple of beers, Mr. Bollywood walked us through soft, dewy grass to a bench carved from a log near a fire-pit blazing under the stars.

Autumn in Austin brought with it cooler nights. Not enough for layers of clothing, but the heat of a roaring fire exuded romance and comfort.

I gave his body a once over and a flood of embarrassment hit me. The way he dashed away from me after the great lipstick debacle, I didn't expect to see him the rest of the night. I thought for sure any chance I had with him was squashed, like my lips against his chest. Hot, rock-solid chest. The man put Adonis to shame. He must be majoring in acting or modeling, or be a jock of some sort with a body like that. Especially after my failed attempt at flirting earlier in the bar, he was way out of my league.

Then by some weird twist of fate he ended up at this party, and my mouth ended up against his body. Not how I planned it, but at least I left an impression. And not just the one of my lips. He'd noticed me enough to come to my rescue when Mr. Gropey Hands hit on me. Though I still wasn't sure if he rescued me or his buddy. Time would tell.

"You cold?" He slid beside me on the log bench.

I shook my head. "Not yet. The fire's cured the chill in the air." *Ugh. Stupid Cat is stupid. I so should have made him cuddle up.*

Orange and yellow flames danced in the breeze rustling through the trees. With each gust, the scent of campfire and cedar surrounded me. The urge to nestle against his chest intensified with each passing moment.

"Just say the word, and I'll make sure you get warmed up." A smile spread over his plump, kissable lips.

I bet. A sly undertone hid among his words. The smolder that burned in his eyes was as bright as the flames in front of us. I prayed his plan included the warmth of his body to keep the chill away. Not to mention it would fall in line with my plans for Project Panty Drop.

I turned to face him. "So, do I get the pleasure of your name, or are you gonna make me guess?"

He clasped his hands together and gave me a half grin. "I like games. I should make you guess. But you'll probably never get it because it's not an American name. I'd rather spend the time getting to know you, than forcing you to spend all night guessing my name."

"What, you're saying I'm not cultured enough to be able to guess your name?" Giving a fake glare, I inched closer to him.

"I said probably. I didn't say absolutely." He winked. "But feel free to give it a shot."

Sliding my fingertip along his torso, I gave a playful poke at his belly. "I think you should have to guess mine first."

He squirmed under my touch, and a full-on grin lit his lips. "Hmm, I think you look like a Katy."

My eyes shot open.

"Hmm, nope. Not Katy. Maybe a Catherine or a Cathy." He shook his head and pursed his lips. "Wait, nope. I got it. You look like a Cat."

My mouth popped open, and I jerked forward on the bench. "How'd you do that?" I narrowed my eyes. "Wait a minute. You already knew my name." With a tilt of my head, I slid closer to him on the bench, pressing my thigh against his with intent. "Were you asking about me?"

He had to have known my name, or asked someone. That meant he was interested. I had him now. He'd be in my pants before the end of the night. Damn, I'd be able to wrap up this term paper by class on Monday.

He threw his head back and let out a laugh. "My little secret, Cat. Now your turn."

"No, you said you would spill your secrets to me over a beer. So out with it, Mr. Bollywood." I gave him my best stern stare, lowering my eyes in a seductive trance as I glanced over the length of his body.

Easing even closer to him, his cologne hit me and sent a heat wave straight to my nether regions. A strong, fresh scent, it reminded me of crisp water, clean and striking. And it made me want to swallow his face with my lips.

Simmer down, Cat. Holy shit!

The man rattled me like no guy I'd ever met.

"Mr. Bollywood?" His eyes danced with delight at the nickname. "I don't know whether to be flattered or offended."

"Choose your own adventure. One will end the night. One will lead to a great beginning. Up to you how you choose to interpret." I leaned into him, tracing the edge of his jeans with my fingernail.

His Adam's apple bounced in his throat. "You're a sly little kitty, aren't you Miss Cat?" Warmth radiated through my fingers as he pressed his thigh against my hand. "I'll let you off the hook this one time. Next time, I'll make you work for it. The name's Jaidev."

I watched his mouth, studying the hard I and hard A, and repeated it in my head over and over.

"But everyone calls me Jai." He scooped my hand and brought it to his lips, gently brushing them across the back of it. A buzz of adrenaline shot through me, and I prayed he didn't feel me shudder. He undid me with a mere touch. Thoughts drifted in my head of what else those lips could do to me.

"Jaidev," I repeated his name in more of a moan than a word.

"You're the first one to actually say it right on the first try. I'm impressed." His fingertip traced little figure eights over the back of my hand now sitting on his thigh. I fought the shiver gnawing at my spine.

The more he touched me the harder it would be to say no to the man should he make it all the way around the bases. I'd love to give him a home run, but the project was a project, and I had to keep thinking of him that way. I already had my online target in play, so I had to get the in-person one tonight. Not to mention, a month had already passed since we got the assignment. It was getting down to the wire.

Plus, I had no intention of sleeping with my target. Just give him enough to want to. But my thoughts drifted to what lay behind those jeans, and I continually had to snap myself out of it.

"Jai, I think I'm getting cold." Nudging myself closer to his lap, I crossed my leg partially onto his.

He swallowed hard, turned his head away, and shot up from the bench. "I'll grab you a sweatshirt or something. Be right back."

I watched him dart away. Dark jeans tightened around his well defined thighs. Each flex of his muscles entranced me as he ran back into the house. "Okay. What the hell just happened?"

JAI

By the time I reached the house I had to stop for breath. Not from running, but from Cat. She stole the air from my lungs. Her sexy glances, and not so subtle movements, had me in a tailspin. It took everything in me not to wrap her up in my arms on that bench. If she weren't the target of my Friend Zone paper, I would have.

Maybe this was a bad idea. Maybe I should find someone else and give Cat a real chance. She didn't seem like the same stuck up snob from the bar. I'd read her all wrong. If she had wanted to blow me off she wouldn't have practically climbed into my lap less than five minutes ago, right?

"Dude, your date's taking up viable sitting room on the

sofa." Mick thumbed over his shoulder. "Wanna get her out of here?"

I shook my head and quirked a brow. "Huh? What the hell are you talking about?"

"Your passed out puke-covered princess," he said with a laugh.

My shoulders slumped as I rolled my eyes. "You honestly don't believe she's here with me, do you? Dude, I'm busy with Cat. Can you please find out who she came with and get her the hell out of here? She's already spilled beer and puked on me. I'm done!"

"Speaking of, how's it going with the Texas Tease?" He folded his arms leaning in the doorway.

My fist clenched at my side. "Jury's still out on that one. Get the hell out of here. I've gotta get back to Cat, and you need to find a home for the vomiting vixen." I ushered him to the front of the house and brushed passed him to the stairs.

I rummaged through my closet and grabbed a sweatshirt. Glancing down at it, I realized just how big of a geek I was. The brown hoodie sported the Serenity logo from the old Joss Whedon show Firefly. She probably wouldn't have the first clue what it was anyway.

With breakneck speed, I shot back down the stairs and made my way through the waning crowd back outside. Someone mentioned a frat house had a party going on at the same time, and from the looks of the thinning herd people were party hopping.

From the doorway, I spied Cat in the arms of some dude I didn't recognize. My seat on the bench didn't stay empty very long. Some jock had his Letterman's jacket draped over her shoulders, and his intentions were made clear as he clutched her to his chest.

Back to Tease status. The chick gave me whiplash. Well, it made it a lot easier to put her back into the target compartment and keep on with Project Friend Zone.

Making a slow stroll, I forced a whistle over my lips to alert them to my incoming presence. Cat jolted up from his chest and stared at me like a deer in headlights. Damn those doe-eyes. They struck me in the heart every time, sending my pulse racing. Must keep to the mission.

"Here you go, Kitty Cat." I offered her the sweatshirt. As she reached for it, I jerked it back. "Oh, but I see you've already been taken care of in my absence."

I turned on my heel, and she shot off the bench and grabbed my arm. "No! It's not what it looks like. Dean just saw me sitting alone and let me borrow his coat 'til you got back."

"That was sure swell of Dean." I tossed the dude an honorable nod.

He threw one back, as if challenging me. "You shouldn't have left her alone."

My jaw clenched. Holding back the adrenaline brewing in my veins, I forced out as even keel of a response as I could muster. "I went to get her a sweater. But you beat me to it. If you'll excuse me, I didn't mean to interrupt."

"You a Browncoat?" Cat questioned.

I spun around nearly making myself dizzy. "Huh?"

She pointed to the sweatshirt. "A Browncoat. A supporter of Joss Whedon's TV show Firefly? I'm part of the Austin Browncoats. Was just wondering if you were, too, since you've got a Serenity sweatshirt and all."

My heart skidded to my stomach. "Yeah. I mean, I'm a Browncoat in general, it's not like I attend meetings or anything. But I love the show and been to a few Can't Stop the Signal events."

Holy Shit. She was a geek! I forced myself from blinking a bazillion times as I stared at her.

"Maybe we could go to one, if you want. There's another event in a couple weeks." She eased herself into the hoodie and sat back on the bench.

"Okay, y'all are geeking way the fuck out. I'm out of here." Dean threw his hands up. "Later." He took off just shy of a sprint back to the house.

I caught her eye roll as Dean left her in the dust. Forcing back a chuckle, I sat next to her on the bench.

"Guess your knight in shining Letterman's couldn't handle the greatness that is Whedon." I crossed a leg to keep some space between us.

Must maintain the cool. Must keep the plan on track. If she weaseled her way against me again, I may not be able to hold back.

Especially after finding out she had a geek side to her. She was going to be the ultimate test of my resolve. But wasn't that what the experiment was all about?

"You surprise me, Jai." A smirk wound itself around her pretty little lips.

"I do?" I stiffened a shoulder as she leaned in.

"I thought you'd be some cocky jock. Turns out you're a pretty cool guy." She traced the length of my forearm with a soft fingertip.

Shivers jolted up and down my spine. I gave her hand a gentle pat with my own to get her to stop. Sucking in a deep breath, I slowed my speeding heart.

"What made you think I was a cocky jock to begin with?" I folded my arms needing to pull away from her roaming fingers.

She shrugged. "I dunno. Saw you at the bar, and you were really into the game. And with a body like yours … " Her gaze trained the length of my body, and I wished it had been her lips rather than her eyes.

"Just what do you mean, a body like mine?" I arched a brow.

Maybe all that working out over the summer paid off. Hell no, I wasn't a jock. I liked football as much as the next guy, but what I had in muscle I lacked in coordination to use them. My strengths came in the form of science fiction and photography, not anything with balls, unless they were my own.

"You must work out a lot." Her fingers traced the edges of the flexed muscles in my folded arms. "So, I figured you must be a football player or something."

I shook my head. "I work out, but I'd rather watch football than play it."

My view inside the house cleared as people continued streaming out. It became a short-lived party when the frat houses had a throw-down.

"The party's dying down. Maybe I should walk you home? We seem to have lost your friend somewhere along the way." I scooted to the edge of the bench, leaning my elbows on my thighs.

Her eyes scanned the perimeter of the yard and house. "I'm sure she found someone to take her to the next party."

"Did you wanna go to the next party? I'm not gonna stop

you if you want some action." Had to think fast, I really had no desire to hit the other party. If I got drunk, I may give into her charms and screw myself out of this project on the first day. "I've gotta hang here. Drew the short straw on the first party of the year, so I got keg and clean up duty this time around. But I can still walk you home if you need me to."

She edged her way next to me, gripping the seat of the bench with both hands as she leaned forward. "Why don't I stay and help you clean up, then you can walk me home. Would suck if I got stuck cleaning this up by my lonesome. I couldn't leave you to the same fate."

I glanced at her with wide eyes. "That's a mighty big gesture. You sure you're up for it? You know not what that all entails."

No matter how bad I wanted in a girl's pants, I don't know that I'd go to the lengths of cleaning a puke covered floor for it. A chick willing to clean up a house after a party had to have ulterior motives.

CHAPTER 4

CAT

Beer soaked into the hem of my skirt from kneeling on the floor trying to grab a red solo cup lodged in a recliner. My clothes reeked like I'd spent a week in a bar. Stale cigarette smoke infused poor Jai's hoodie. It wouldn't be right to give it back to him smelling like the bottom of an ashtray.

What the hell was I thinking when I volunteered to help him clean up? Clearly, I wasn't. My vajayjay did the talking at that particular moment, and I could kick her ass for it.

"I think I got most of it cleaned up in here." Not watching where I was going, I slid on something across the tile floor and right into Jai's arms.

"Whoa there! If you wanted to fall into my arms all you had to do was ask." He winked.

My heart careened through my chest. He held me effortlessly, suspended above the floor as if we floated. Our eyes locked, and I said a silent prayer for his lips to brush mine. Instead, both of our noses twitched as the scent of stale beer and intestinal contents hit us at the same time.

"I think I'm gonna hurl." I covered my mouth.

"Me too, let's get out of here." He scooped me into his arms and carried me out of the room, easing me onto the bottom stair.

"I still smell it." My face cringed and crinkled as I tried to take a breath not saturated by the horrendous odor. "I think it's on my clothes."

"Here, why don't you wash off. I'll give you something to change into. I'll go clean up the rest of the room, and then I'll take you home. You shouldn't have to be subjected to this." He guided me up the stairs to his room.

After rummaging through his closet, he handed me a t-shirt and a pair of shorts. "You'll drown in them, but it'll be enough to get you back to your dorm somewhat clothed. There's towels and washcloths in the bathroom. Help yourself. I promise they're all clean."

"Thanks." His gorgeous smile lured me in, and I stared at him, hoping I didn't drool.

"Bathroom's across the hall. I'll be back in a few minutes." He ducked out the door.

After a spit-shine bath and a change of clothes, I finally managed a full breath of clean air again. Back in Jai's room, I took inventory of what few items decorated the room. Like a true UT student, burnt orange plastered his walls, from banners to ball caps. The longhorn logo was a clear staple in his interior design scheme.

I slid open his closet. Several nice dress shirts hung neatly on hangers, along with pressed slacks. At least he wasn't a slob. In the back though, several old t-shirts peeked from the depths. Thumbing through them, my heart fluttered. All kinds of old sci-fi shirts pressed together in a mash at the back; gaming ones, old TV shows from Star Wars to Star Trek, and comic book heroes. The guy had a definite secret nerdy side he was trying to keep hidden. And it hit my soft spot, hard.

After closing the closet door, I made my way through the rest of the room. A picture sat on his bedside table of him and some gorgeous woman with stunning exotic eyes and salon perfect hair. I hoped and prayed it was a family member and not his girlfriend or something. The more I thought about it, the more I wanted to draw a sharpie 'stache on her. Jealousy nipped at my heart, and I shook it off.

I wandered to his desk and noticed a notebook open by his

laptop. The top page had my sociology professor's name on it. Odd, Jai wasn't in my class. As I inspected further, the outline of our class term projects stared me in the face. He *was* in my class. But how? Was he taking it online or something?

Panic ransacked my stomach as I read his notes further. Project Friend Zone—How a male can remain friends with a female he finds attractive. Then the kicker, next to it he scrawled my name.

That asshat! He was using me.

Short bursts of air huffed in and out of my chest as I processed the words in front of me. Here I thought he had been some sort of gentleman; with the sweater, swooping in to save me, our almost kiss in the kitchen. All of it a set up. My nails stung the flesh of my palm as my hand curled to a fist.

Then regret bitch-slapped me back to reality. I'd been using him all along though, too. Project Panty Drop.

I glanced down at the Avengers t-shirt he'd given me to wear, and a pair of shorts I had to knot three times to get them to stay up on my hips. A sneaky grin slid across my lips as an idea popped into my head. This just became a game, and one I wouldn't lose. I slid myself out of my bra and shoved it into the plastic bag he'd given me to put my smelly clothes in.

I hiked the t-shirt up, knotting it at my side so it tightened around my breasts before giving each a slow twirl with my fingers, turning their headlights on high beam. Loosening the knots on his shorts, I let them droop, hanging low on my hips. I shucked out my hair and let it drape around me like a cloak.

A knock on the door sent my heart racing.

"Cat, are you decent?" Jai said behind the door.

"I'm fully clothed if that's what you mean," I replied. Decent was debatable at the moment as I set my plan in motion.

He walked in and jerked to a stop. His chest puffed out as his mouth popped open.

Mission accomplished.

"Um." His attention glued to my bosom then shot to my face. "I completely forgot what I was gonna say." He brushed a hand through his hair, and it got stuck midway. Squinted eyes replaced his previously wide ones as he squished up his face. "Shit.

I need a shower. Don't even tell me what just got stuck in my hair."

I shook my head with a half-cocked smile. Heat blossomed in my belly the moment my eyes caught sight of his flexed muscles. His t-shirt stretched to the limits around his olive skin. Out of the corner of my eyes, I caught his nose in an adorable crinkle as he grimaced. He was nothing short of adorkable.

"Give me ten minutes to shower, and I promise I'll get you out of here." He dashed to his closet, and reached for another pair of jeans and t-shirt.

"Trying to get rid of me?" I folded my arms over my chest, forgetting my previous mission. My skin brushed over my stiff nipples, and I dropped my arms to my sides. Mustn't hide my secret weapons when I needed them most.

Throwing a little swagger in my hips, I sauntered over to him and drug a nail down the middle of his Captain America t-shirt. He swallowed hard and choked back a cough.

As I pressed against him, the scent of cigarettes and throw up hit me, and I wretched. Clasping a hand over my face, I jerked back from him. "Yeah, I think a shower's in order. I'll just wait right here."

His cheeks colored like a glass of Merlot as he tore out of the room and slammed the door to the bathroom across the hall.

I shot over to his desk and thumbed through his notebook scouring for info on his 'Friend Zone' plan. Nothing solid. Looked like he'd only just begun to plot. Maybe I'd thrown him for enough of a loop to catch him. Time would tell. Until then, Project Panty Drop was in full swing.

JAI

Those nips stared at me, all but inviting me to lunge at them with my lips. As I sudsed myself, my hand worked its way to my dick, aching for release. Just like her tits tight under my shirt. My shirt. I'd never wash it. Her prefect upturned breasts filled it out. And the way my shorts all but fell off her fuckable hips, I could practically taste her as I slammed my hand against the shower wall, shuddering as I came.

I huffed through a series of terse breaths, slowing my heart rate back to normal. Getting myself off would definitely help when it came time to kiss her later. She'd expect it once we got back to her dorm. She wanted me. And fuck if I didn't want her. The next couple days would be all hand jobs until I got this paper done.

I was sure she'd give up after I ignored all her advances. Shouldn't be more than a couple more days, tops. I'd have my paper done well before the end of the semester. One less thing I had to think about before India.

Shit. India. The trip had been planned for years. My family expected it. While my folks grew up in Mumbai as children, they moved to London after they were married. The rest of our family still lived in India. And the fact that I hadn't married, and I was twenty-two, didn't sit well with them. Arranged marriages still happened. More than I wanted to think about. Even as India moved to become more modern, it clung tight to cultural ideals it had held sacred for centuries.

Glad I thought about that after I jacked off, such a mood killer.

I made my way back to my room, finding Cat lying on my bed. A gasp lodged in my throat as my eyes trailed over her body, fixating on the patch of exposed skin around her belly. My shorts barely swaddled her hips, giving me short of a neon flashing sign that the girl was no stranger to a Brazilian wax. Heat swarmed my jeans. So much for getting the job done ahead of time.

Think about India. Think about India.

My jeans relaxed, letting lose their grip on my cock. I blew out a breath and instantly regretted it. She knew she got to me. The sexy smile curling her kissable lips practically spanked me.

"Tired?" I managed to choke out as air filtered back into my lungs.

"Not anymore." She pushed herself up as she rested her

hands behind her for balance.

"Good, cause I'm not sure what dorm you're in so I'll need you to guide me." *Take that you sexy siren. I ain't falling for it.*

The shock on her face gave me instant gratification. I'd blown her out of the water. It took everything in me not to fist pump my victory.

She eased herself off the bed and stalked toward me. "God, you smell good. What is that you're wearing?" Her tongue darted between her lips, slicking them in a seductive sheen that nearly stopped my heart.

"Soap," I choked out an octave higher than I'd intended.

Tilting her head, she inched her way to her tiptoes, stretching her way to my mouth. Shit.

India. India. India.

Thank God she was short. If she'd been any taller and made contact, my restraint might have left me. Luckily, I'd have to bend down to kiss her.

India. India. India.

She grabbed my shirt and yanked me down toward her.

Whiskey. Tango. Foxtrot. India.

She was stronger than she looked and yanked me too hard. I toppled over her, and we thumped to the floor in a tangled mass of arms and legs. We peeled ourselves off each other, and she covered her face with her hands. My heart lurched to my throat. I felt like the biggest ass on the planet. If she only knew just how much I really wanted to kiss her.

"I'm such a complete klutz. Sorry, I lost my footing." I hoped to take the embarrassment off her and put it on me.

"You?" Her lashes fluttered. "I slipped on the hardwood floor and grabbed onto you."

A chuckle popped from her throat. One escaped mine as well. We laughed at the ridiculousness of it as we untwisted the remainder of our limbs.

"I need to find my shoes. I think I kicked them under your bed when we fell." Crawling on her hands and knees, her stunning ass stared me in the face. She lunged forward, grabbing a shoe, then pushed back, shoving her tight and toned cheeks back at me. That little minx. Cute, klutzy, and so full of sexy all at the same time. I prayed there wasn't a puddle of drool at my feet.

"Got 'em." She slid back, sitting on her haunches.

"Here, let me help you." I stared at the sexy black pumps. "These aren't made for walking."

"Well, I hadn't planned on having to walk back to my dorm tonight. Angie ditched me, and she was my ride." She shrugged.

"Guess I'll have to drive you then. What hall are you in?" I pushed myself to a stance and offered her a hand.

She slipped her petite hand in mine, and the softness of her skin undid me. Goosebumps shot up my arms, riding the shiver all the way down my back. Her big whiskey eyes pulled me in, and I leaned forward, finding myself chest to chest with her.

"I'm in San Jacinto Hall." Her words shocked me back to reality as her warm breath tickled my lips.

I reached behind her for my keys on the desk. Sucking in a deep breath, I closed my eyes. *If I don't get an A on this fucking paper, I'm quitting school.*

CHAPTER 5

CAT

Silence dominated the majority of our drive back to my dorm hall. Jai seemed awfully tense. Maybe it pissed him off he had to drive me. But he offered. It's not like I begged him to. His hands twisted on the steering wheel until his skin squeaked against the plastic.

None of my flirting had busted his resolve. The man had a stronger will than I gave him credit for. Maybe it was a cultural thing. I'd have to do some investigating into his ethnicity. Hell, I'd have to do some investigating on him period. I had no clue if he grew up here in the states, or if he grew up in India. He had no discernible accent, barely a hint of some kind of maybe British influence, which led me to believe he'd been here for quite a while, if not born here.

Maybe he grew up more prim and proper, and he had to be the one to make the first moves. Clearly, I got to him in some shape or form, but the depths of which I had yet to find out. I studied him every time I made an attempt, and his body language spoke volumes over his words.

"So, what else do you do for fun, besides roll in vomit and cigarettes?" I gave him a soft smile, trying to break the uneasy silence.

He let out a hearty laugh. The sound of it swelled through my ears and warmed my heart. "I like video games, football, and cooking." His stiffened shoulders eased, and he rested his wrist on the top of the steering wheel releasing his hulk-like death grip. "You?"

"Oh, wow, you cook?" I crossed my legs and ran the length of them with my fingers.

With a quick shrug, he gave my legs the side-eye. "Yeah. If I didn't, we'd all starve at the house. Or live on frozen pizza and beer. My mom is a great cook, and I used help her in the kitchen."

As if he didn't come off adorable enough, the man liked to cook. And he loved his mother. Ugh. My ovaries puffed and exploded.

"What about you?" He tossed me another glance before returning his attention to the road.

"I like to read. I'm a sucker for sci-fi and fantasy. And some comic books. I've even written some fan-fic." Could I have sounded more like a dweeb with no life? I wondered if I pulled my sonic screwdriver from my purse, if he'd get a hard-on or push me out of the car.

"Cool." The hum of the car engine drown out his whisper. He cleared his throat. "Here we go. San Jac Hall, m'lady."

He shot me another side-eyed glance, and his hand tightened around the steering wheel once more. The man had tells. He bolted out of the car before I managed to utter a thank you. Opening my door, he offered his hand and eased me out.

"Old-fashioned are we, Mr. Bollywood?" I shot him a wink.

"That would be Mr. Sankar. And, well, a part of me is anyway." He leaned against the car, folding his arms the length of his broad chest.

A five o'clock shadow stubbled his chiseled jawline. An ache welled in me to run my hand along it, itching to feel the prickles of the hairs under my fingertips. Streaks of silver moonlight shone in his dark hair. Soft, dreamy eyes stared back at me.

"Well, goodnight, Mr. Sankar. I'd be lying if I said I enjoyed myself tonight. But there were a few redeeming moments in our adventures." I gave a tilt to my head, biting the bottom of my lip.

"I could make it up to you if you want to come back over

tomorrow and watch a little football. I assume you like it, since you were sitting in the bar today watching the UT game."

I knew it. He'd been watching me. He must have asked around and found out my name. But if he was interested, why would he choose me for his stupid Friend Zone sociology project? A twinge hit my heart.

"I could make that happen. What time?" Inching myself closer, he had nowhere to run pinned between me and his car.

"Noon," he murmured in a slow slide down the door.

His words turned into an soft moan. Thankfully my attention had been focused on his handsome mouth, and I read his lips.

"Noon it shall be," I said, a breath away from his mouth.

He shot to a complete stance, towering over my five-foot-four-inch frame, leaving me unable to reach him for a kiss. "I promise I'll air out the house tonight and invest in some air freshener."

"Much appreciated." I pursed my lips. He foiled my advances once again. "What about coming to my dorm to watch it? Fewer people, less stink."

His Adam's apple bounced in his throat. "Already promised the guys I'd grill out. They request my kabobs every Sunday. You're in for a real treat."

I bet. I'd love to lick his kabob.

"All right then, noon it is. Goodnight, Jaidev." I let out a sigh and gave him a glance over my shoulder as I walked up to the hall.

"Sweet dreams, Kitty Cat." He tossed a wave and a beaming smile as he walked back to the driver's side of the car and slid in.

My loud clackety stomps down the hall got me the stink-eye from some of the other residents. I stalked my way back to my room and threw myself on my bed. The man infuriated me. I'd have to step up my game tomorrow. I wasn't about to drag this out. I'd give him another day, tops, before he crumbled.

JAI

My head fell against my hands, holding tight to the steering wheel. A long, heated breath blew from my lips, emptying out the last of the frustration I'd sucked into my lungs. I hardly knew anything about her. I'd never had such pure, intense sexual attraction to a girl. Even to the ones I dated. Sure, there was some form of attraction or I wouldn't have bothered. But none that set me on fire with such a carnal desire without even having kissed her yet.

Tomorrow may be another story. I didn't know how much longer I could hold out. I needed to end this completely, or just have sex with her. In less than twenty-four hours she'd spun my world upside down. She had no idea she was mere seconds from my hands raking her body, claiming her. The girl threw herself at me, begging for me to free her of the stupid geeky shirt I'd given her to wear. Nothing had ever looked sexier to me.

I'd have to find another Friend Zone target. One I was still attracted to, but one I'd have a better chance at holding out for. Tomorrow, Cat would be mine.

I put the car in drive as something caught my eye on the passenger seat. She'd left her purse. I huffed a breath, wondering if she'd done it on purpose. My resolve may not make it to tomorrow. Summoning the last bit of my will power, I grabbed her purse and headed up to her dorm. Only I had no idea which room she was in. Nor had I gotten her phone number.

A buxom blonde came at me from the foyer, bra-less. I thought for sure she'd give herself a black eye with the way they all but bounced out of her night shirt. I knew I was a goner the moment I didn't get stiff from it. Cat already had me whipped. Shit.

"Excuse me," I said as she closed in on me.

"You need no excuse, sexy. All you have to say is please." She threw a hand on her hip and licked her lips with a seductive smile.

Instead of turning me on, it completely turned me off. In fact, it skeeved me out a little. At one point in time I'd have thrown her against the wall, got a little action and then proceeded to find

Cat. Now, all I wanted was to give Cat her purse and ravage the hell out of her.

"Please, can you help me find Cat Marek? She left her purse in my car." My eyes smiled at her the minute Cat's name left my lips.

Her face drooped, and her hand slipped off her hip. "Third floor. I think room three-fifteen."

I grabbed her hand and dotted the back of it with a quick kiss. "Thank you."

Her lips slithered back to a sly grin as she brushed past me. "My room is one-ten, if you're interested." She sauntered off before the word no ever left my lips.

I stepped off the elevator and Mick's voice caught me off guard. Peeking around the corner, I caught sight of him helping a dark-blonde stay upright against the wall. If he was looking to score tonight, he picked the wrong chick. She'd pass out on him before she ever got her legs open.

"I like you," she slurred. "I'd never do what my roomie's doing, ya know."

He fumbled with a set of keys trying to unlock her door. "Oh yeah? What's that?"

"She's using him for a soc … soci … for a fucking term paper. Teasing him into sleeping with her. But I'd never do that." Her back slid down the wall, and Mick dove to catch her.

Propping her up on his chest, he fought with the lock again. "Easy there, Angie. I think it's time for you to get some sleep."

She licked her lips and clung to his shoulder. "I'd rather have sex. Maybe we should go back to your house. Cat may be in there having sex with Mr. Bollywood."

A lump wadded in my throat. Cat was using me. I pressed my back against the wall, raking my hand through my hair. Here I thought she was genuinely interested. I even passed up on getting some easy ass downstairs because I wanted only Cat. I almost gave up on my own term paper to be with her.

Well shit.

It hit me—I was using her too. Less than five seconds away from blowing it all, too, just to tell her I wanted to make a go of it. I could've kicked my own ass for that one. My fingers curled, leaving my knuckles white. I shook my head and let out a huff.

Operation Friend Zone just kicked into high gear. I marched down the hall, gripping Cat's purse like a lifeline.

"Having trouble?" I asked Mick, stopping behind him.

"Hey, Jai. Yeah, can you help a guy out?" He nodded toward Angie. "Trying to get her to bed before she yaks on me."

"Did you try knocking? I think Cat's inside." I gave the door a light rap with my knuckles.

Moments later the door creaked open, snapped back by the chain. Cat's eyes flashed wide open as she shut the door and unlocked the chain before reopening it.

"What's going on?" Her wide doe-eyes shot a zing through my heart. I had to find a way to counter that. Damn those fucking eyes of hers.

"Mick's trying to get your roomie safely home. Care to let us in?" I gave her my best smile.

"Of course." She opened the door wider, fanning her arm towards the inside.

Mick swung Angie up in his arms and carried her to the bed.

"She okay?" Cat asked, hitching up to her tiptoes to see over his shoulder.

"Drunk off her ass. I tried to stop her at the frat party, but she decided to do kegstands with the big boys. Girl's got balls. Well, I hope not real ones. She's kinda cute. But still, I don't think she's gonna feel good in the morning. May wanna keep a trash can handy." Mick tucked her in and tossed me a wave. "Later, dude. I'll see ya back at the house."

I gave him a nod as he left then turned to Cat. "Brought your purse back. You forgot it in my car."

Her eyes lit up as a smile curled over those pouty kissable lips of hers. "Aren't you just the gentleman?"

At one time I was. Now, the war was on. I planned on being the winner. "I've been called that a time or two." I inched closer to her, lifting her chin with my fingertip. "I guess I'll see you tomorrow then."

Her lips popped open, waiting for my next move. Her lids pressed closed, and a sly grin spread across my face as I pulled away and left her there, shutting the door behind me.

CHAPTER 6

CAT

I opened my eyes. He was gone. My tongue pushed against the back of my clenched teeth and my fingernails pressed crescent moons into my fleshy palms.

He was good. But I was better. And I planned on proving it tomorrow.

A puff of aggravated breath huffed from my lungs as I plunked down at my computer. I logged into my messenger hoping WhoDat would be on to take my mind off things. No such luck.

To distract myself, I typed up some notes on my project thus far, denoting Jai's reactions and lack thereof. Specifically detailing I knew that he was also doing a paper on me. We'd see who came out the winner.

A yawn escaped my lips, and as I closed the lid on my laptop my messenger dinged.

WhoDat: You still up?

Me: There you are. I was wondering where you were. I guess your shindig went well.

WhoDat: You were wondering about me?

Me: Maybe.

A twinge of regret flooded me as I hit send. It was the first time I'd crossed over that line with him in chat, giving him any indication I wanted more than just friendly geek-related conversation. I wondered if he'd take the bait.

WhoDat: I was wondering about you, too. Shindig was kind of a bust, and wanted to check to see if maybe you were on. I'm just glad the night ended on a better note.

Me: It did? How so?

WhoDat: I caught you online.

Oh, that sly guy. A tiny flutter stirred in my heart. Part of me wished I knew what he looked like. But, for the sake of my project, I had to keep it strictly conversation based for now.

Me: I'm flattered. I kind of like this new side of you.

WhoDat: What side would that be, Impossible Girl?

My heart lunged to my stomach. What if I misread his message and he just wanted to ask me a question or something? Here I thought he had been flirting back with me. Maybe he wasn't.

Me: I'm hoping it's a flirtatious one.

Silence. I stared at the blinking cursor, willing it to present me with a message. Angie's snoring snapped me back to reality, and I glanced over my shoulder. Turning my attention back to my messenger, I sat still, waiting for a response.

WhoDat: Do you want me to flirt with you?

I pursed my lips. What kind of a response was that? I bit my bottom lip as I formulated a reply.

Me: You wear coy like a shirt, sir.

WhoDat: How do you know I'm a sir?

Shit. Oh. My. God. What if it's a chick? My lashes fluttered at the speed of light as I processed the thought. I just naturally assumed.

Me: I don't. I must admit, I kind of like the anonymity of it all.

My heart sped to the point it made me dizzy. Holy crap, what if he was a she? I ran a hand through my hair as I fought to catch my breath. I honestly didn't know what to do if he turned out to be a she.

WhoDat: Do you wanna know the truth? Or keep it a secret interlude?

Me: It would make cybersex difficult if I don't know what body parts you have.

WhoDat: Wow, this conversation certainly took an interesting turn.

Me: That it did. Do you regret it did?

Part of me regretted it. Part of me tingled with excitement. We were about to pass the point of no return. I feared losing my friendship with him/her, but every thought about making it more sent a flutter to my belly.

WhoDat: I regret nothing. Except the fact that I can't

see your face to look into your eyes. I imagine them sweet and sultry, inviting me in as I close in on your soft lips.

My pulse shot to an all-time high. Holy Shit. I'd never cybered with anyone before. I was kinda sorta kidding when I mentioned it. I didn't think he—she'd be into it. Fear numbed my fingers and my typing skills fell by the wayside.

Me: They're brown. Yours?

WhoDat: Brown as well. Deep brown. Full lips? Are they pouty and kissable?

I'd never thought about it before. I shot up to my bathroom and took a glance in the mirror. Tilting my head, I studied their shape running a finger along them. I darted back to my chair.

Me: Like pillows, soft and supple.

WhoDat: Nice. Very nice. I can practically taste them. Imagine me pulling them between my own lips, tracing them with my tongue before sweeping your gorgeous mouth into a deep kiss. Sliding my tongue over yours in a delicious dance. The things I would do to that mouth. Like sucking your supple lips between my teeth. You're getting me very hot, Impossible Girl.

And he/she was me. My heart hammered against my ribcage, and heat zinged between my legs. I was dying to know if it was a him or a her. I typed out the question, but just as quick deleted it.

Me: I'd punish your wandering tongue, forcing it back with my own, deepening the kiss as I dug my nails into your flesh, aching for more of you. To feel your skin against mine, heated and tingling. I'd massage my fingers through your hair to the rhythm of our kisses. Tugging at your lips with my own, begging for more.

This naughty and rebellious side turned into an exhilarating high. Did this count as getting him/her into my pants if we had cybersex? No, I had to get him/her to meet in person. But damn, if this didn't quench my thirst for Jai right now. In fact, I pictured WhoDat as him, for the sake of the moment.

WhoDat: You're making me extremely hot, Impossible Girl. My hands are wandering my body thinking of you, wishing it was you wrapping your hand around my cock.

PEEN! YES! Oh thank God. While I'd kissed a girl or two in my college years, I really preferred penis.

Me: Are you sliding your hand along it with long, tight strokes, up and down the entire length? Wet your fingers, pretend it's my lips clinging to your flesh, pulling it in and out of my lips.

Heat pooled beneath me, and I needed new panties. An ache welled up in me, the need to stroke myself as I read our words. My clit twinged between my legs, begging for a release.

WhoDat: I wish I could hear your voice, whispering these things to me. You're making my cock hard as a rock, IG. Damn.

The slight problem with that—I didn't whisper. And I hated it when other people did.

Me: I would, but my roomie's here, and I don't want her to hear.

WhoDat: Maybe another time? I'd love to hear you moan, thinking about my fingers tracing your clit, sliding between your lower lips. I've got long fingers, IG, great for plunging in and out of your tight pussy.

Me: You're making me moan right now. I'm aching to touch myself. Begging for it to be your hands gripping tight to my breasts, my nipples hardening between your fingers. I'd rock my hips over your hand, stroking moans from my lips, screaming your name. I wanna know your name.

WhoDat: Not tonight. Tonight, we're wearing masks ... a sensual, sexual hidden dance, IG. Maybe sometime in person I'll get you to scream my name as I'm plunging into you with my hard cock. Holding your perfect breasts in my hands, taking you from behind, claiming you, filling you with pleasure until you crumble in my arms, and I take you to bed and eat and drink from your perfect pink pussy. I wanna hear you whimper as you orgasm in my arms, knowing I'm the one who made you do so.

As I read his words one hand drifted to my breast, pinching my own nipple until it pebbled in my fingertips. The other slipped into my underwear, running the length of my slit drenched in my arousal. Holy shit did he get me wet. My breathing turned ragged and fast as the sensations built with each swipe of my fingertips. Short puffs of air shot in and out of my lungs as the waves of my orgasm pummeled me, and I rocked against my hand in the chair.

Angie moaned and rolled over letting out a loud snore, scaring the shit out of me.

WhoDat: I know you just came.

Me: How do you know I came?

WhoDat: Because I just did. And you took a while to respond. :) I'd love to see your face in theafterglow.

Hold you in my arms and just stare into your eyes.

Me: You don't even know what I look like. What if I'm hideous?

WhoDat: I highly doubt you're hideous. We've talked for a while now and you're the sweetest, funniest girl I've ever met online. You're intelligent, and you have great taste in geekery. What if I'm the hideous one?

Me: You are the first guy to get me to have cybersex. I highly doubt you're hideous either. The things you said, you knew exactly what to say to get me to touch myself without me even realizing it. You make me feel pretty.

WhoDat: I just want you to know, I wasn't expecting to do this tonight. I was actually just looking to talk to you. Had a kind of bummer of a night, and you always make me smile.

My heart pooled in my chest. Sexy and sweet. He had me falling for him. Shit. A twinge of guilt hit me. I needed to call it off. I needed to find someone else. I couldn't break his heart. He was already breaking mine with his words.

Me: I wasn't expecting it either. I had kind of a bummer of a night, too, and needed a release. I don't know what got into me.

WhoDat: Hopefully no one else until I can. ;)

Me: LOL Should I put a lock on my pussy until I see you?

WhoDat: Yes. I just claimed it. But I want the rest of you, too.

Me: Keep saying stuff like that and it's all yours.

WhoDat: You wear me out, Impossible Girl. I need sleep now. Someday I'll wake up, and you'll be in my arms. Sweet Dreams.

Me: I'd like that. Sweet Dreams.

My heart skipped. An emptiness filled me watching his name gray out as he signed off. Tracing his name on my screen with a fingertip, I bit my lip and let out a sigh. I, too, needed sleep. I had to deal with Jai tomorrow. Suddenly, I didn't even want to do the paper anymore. I feared I was getting in far too deep. I hadn't planned on falling for either of them. But it was due in a couple weeks, and I had no idea what else to do it on.

I crawled into bed and lost myself in thoughts about WhoDat as I replayed the conversation in my head, finding my hands wandering back to my panties.

CHAPTER 7

CAT

The red, white, and blue Texans jersey hugged my cleavage in all the right places, and I was thankful they now came tailored to a woman's body. My old standard Packers Jersey, while sentimental, hung over me like a tent. Not what I needed to lure Jai in.

I draped a low ponytail on either side of my shoulders, channeling the pseudo-schoolgirl look. Complete with boy shorts and Mary Janes, I'd hopefully knock his socks off. Or even better, his pants.

Throwing a glance over my shoulder to Angie sawing logs in her bunk, I headed out the door. I had thirty minutes to get to Jai's house, purposely walking so he'd have to drive me back again tonight.

Warm late-October sunshine blazed on my skin, and I regretted not bringing my sunglasses. The warm fall weather was one of the reasons I chose UT in the first place. I needed out of the frozen tundra of Wisconsin. I loathed that I had to sport a Texans jersey instead of a Packer one, but I took one for the team and my term paper. I hoped Aaron Rodgers would forgive me this once.

I rang the bell on the front of the house, and Jai answered

the door in record time. "Is it safe to come in?"

"I promise, it's puke free." He stood back to let me in.

Charcoal smoke filled the room through the open windows. The smell of hamburger grease wafted up my nose, along with beer and whatever else they had dripping over the grill.

"Much better than last night." My belly rumbled a loud growl that even I heard, and blood rushed to my cheeks. Great, he'll probably think I've got gas or something.

"Better get you fed, Kitty Cat. Don't want you hulking out on us." He slid his hand over mine, and a tingle shimmied straight to my toes curling in my Mary Janes. He had soft hands for a guy. I needed to remember to ask what he moisturized with.

"Smells divine." I eyed a layer of skewered meat and veggies covering the grate of the grill.

"My specialty kabobs." After plating some food, he swept my hand in his and guided us back inside to the couch.

Several guys wandered in and out of the room carrying large plates with mountains of food. The big screen in the front room tuned in to the Texans game. I plunked down on one of the three sofas lining the walls.

"At least you have good taste in beer." I sipped my cup of Shiner Bock before setting it down on one of the end tables that wedged between the couches.

"We don't like drinking piss water," Mick said from the sofa across from me.

"Me either. In fact, I don't drink anything I can see through. The darker the better for me." Crossing a leg, I worked to balance my plate on my lap.

"My kinda girl." Jai slid next to me on the sofa, just about dumping the contents of my plate into my lap. Rushing to catch it, my fingers gripped the plate before it tipped. "Good ninja-like reflexes. Nice save."

I pursed my lips as I forced the chunks of chicken and bell peppers back onto my plate. "I had several brothers growing up. I've had a lot of practice."

"Did you grow up in Texas?" He asked before shoving just about an entire skewer into his mouth.

I shook my head, managing a dainty bite of my chicken.

"Nope. Wisconsin."

"Wow, what brought you all the way down here?" He scarfed down the last of his food. Damn the man could put it away. I supposed he worked it off in order to maintain a body like that.

"I got tired of the cold. I miss snow on Christmas and that's about it. You?"

"Born in India. But we moved to London when I was a baby. Then my dad started his own practice here in the states, and we moved when I was ten. Been here ever since. What, you couldn't tell by my accent?"

I could never pick up accents, but staring at his mouth, I noticed the formation of some words were just a bit off. His precision was different. I'd catch certain words he'd say with a bit of a sexy lilt that sent flutters to my belly.

"Interesting. Have you been back to India at all?"

With shoulders slumped, his brow furrowed, and he forced his lips to a thin line. "Yeah, we went over there for my sister's wedding a couple years ago. Supposed to go back over winter break. It's a long story. Not really looking forward to it."

Odd. I'd think a trip to see long lost family would be exciting, especially out of the country. But dread shadowed his eyes the moment I brought the subject up.

"I'm guessing you don't wanna talk about it." I set my plate on the end table and turned to face him.

He shook his head. "Not right now. I need to just chill and watch the game, if you don't mind."

I gave a nod and inched my way closer on the sofa. He shot out of his seat and grabbed my plate. "Need a refill before kickoff?"

Narrowing my eyes, I gave him a sly stare. I'd get in his lap one way or another. "Yeah, I'll take another beer. I'm full up on food though. The kabobs were fantastic."

"Thanks. Glad you enjoyed them. Be right back." He jogged out of the room.

My phone buzzed, and I ripped open my purse. The anticipation in my heart sunk deep when the email address read Angie and not WhoDat. I thought maybe he'd email me after our heated exchange last night. We'd given each other our email addresses shortly after we started talking, but we never sent anything, only spoke via messenger. A brief thought filtered through my brain about emailing him, but I didn't want to seem needy or stalkery. I had to let him come to me.

Balancing several beers in his arms, Jai passed them to the other guys before handing me one.

"So, you're a Texans fan?" He asked taking a long chug from his cup.

I shrugged. "Sort of. I figure as long as I'm in Texas I should be. But my heart belongs to the Packers. Die Hard Lifer."

He gave a nod. "Yeah, Aaron Rodgers is killer."

"Along with Clay Matthews, Jordy Nelson—" I said, but he held up a hand to stop me.

His smile spread wider on his face. "Wow, a chick who actually knows their names and doesn't refer to them by 'that hot guy in tight pants'. I'm impressed."

Folding my arms, I shot him a glare that could melt the polar ice caps. "Well I'm glad I upped your low opinion of me."

His shoulder hitched. "Hey, I'm only kidding. I just know a lot of girls who 'pretend' to like football to get into a guy's pants."

"I actually eat, drink, and sleep football. So, shut up cause the game's starting." I nudged him in the side with my elbow, and he squirmed, throwing an arm above my head on the couch.

Giving him a side-eyed glance, a smile curled on my lips. The Texans scored, and we both leapt off the sofa in a cheer. As I came back down, I crashed against his lap, and his arms wrapped around me.

His cologne hit me like a wave, sending my head spinning. The urge to nuzzle his neck and inhale more of him overwhelmed me. I leaned back, and he held me to his chest, resting his chin on the top of my head.

Why didn't he friend zone me? Maybe I'd indeed broken through his barriers.

His arms tightened around my waist, clasping together against my stomach. Muscles in his arms stiffened as he lost himself in the game, hitching with every sack and incomplete pass. By half-time his cologne seeped into my jersey.

He eased me from his lap. "Need to use the head. Want

anything while I'm up?"

That was a loaded question, and I held back a snort as I shook my head. "I'm okay for now."

As he jogged up the stairs, I caught him tossing me a glance. I forced back the smile on my lips and took my phone from my purse, needing a social media break.

By the time half-time was over, Jai still hadn't returned. Maybe his kabobs got to him. My phone dinged, signaling an incoming email. Flutters attacked my belly when WhoDat popped up in my email inbox. I forced out tiny breaths, working to get my racing heart under control.

"You okay?" Jai asked as he plunked next to me on the sofa, wrapping his arm around my back.

"Yeah." Engrossed in the fact WhoDat emailed me, I never noticed Jai come back down the stairs. "Um, I think it's my turn to use the facilities. Is it safe to use yours upstairs, or do you have another?"

He quirked a brow. "I was … on the phone … with my mom. It's safe for human habitation, I assure you, but you can use the one down here if you want."

I made my way to the restroom. Whipping out my phone, I swiped my email inbox scrolling for his name.

> Hey Impossible Girl,
>
> Just thinking about you, hoping you're having a good day. I admit I'm also thinking about our conversation from last night. I'm busy for the next couple of hours, but I'm all yours tonight if you've got nothing going on. We could watch a Who episode online together and see where things lead us. Shoot me a line if you're up for it.
>
> WD
>
> *P.S. I hope you bought a lock.*

It took everything in me to hold back the squee bottling up

in my throat. It would probably be in be in bad form if I Kermit Flailed around his bathroom.

> Hey WD,
>
> My day just got a whole lot better. Consider it a date. I should be home by six. If you're good tonight, maybe I'll mail you the key.
>
> Impossible Girl

Giving myself a once over in the mirror, I made my way back out where the guys sat, eyes still glued to the TV. No one even noticed I was gone. As I got to the sofa, a smile so big it could light up the room beamed from Jai's face. And it wasn't for me. Nose deep in his phone, he more than likely read up on how best to stick it to me friend-wise. Must've been a fantastic idea, and a twinge of fear stabbed at my heart.

"Did I miss anything?" I said, easing myself next to him on the sofa.

He jerked back as if I startled him. "Um, I dunno. I wasn't paying attention. Got a message from my best friend." Shoving the phone back into his pocket, he opened his arms and beckoned me to sit back on his lap.

"I thought Mick was your best friend? You often message each other in the same room?"

A snort snapped from his throat. "No. A different best friend. Someone I grew up with."

I didn't trust him. Quirking a brow, I nestled into his arms, but the Texans scored a touchdown and he all but launched me back across the room with a fist pump.

He lunged at me, making sure I was all right. "Oh my God! I'm so sorry."

"I'm fine." I adjusted myself as he eased me back to a stance.

My phone vibrated again, and I welcomed the momentary distraction. A wide smile spread over my own lips as I read WD's response.

What do I get if I'm great? Perhaps a pic of my prize? Maybe a phone call?

I choked back a giggle as I typed. My heart raced at the thought of emailing WD and standing in the room with Jai. Just thinking about my conversation with WD heated my nethers to near boiling.

Prize to be determined upon number of orgasms achieved.

"Looks like the Texans will pull it off. Two minute warning and they're ahead 21 to 10. You okay to turn it off or do you wanna keep watching?" Jai asked.

"Hmm?" I whipped around, shoving my phone into my purse.

He nodded his head toward the stairs. "Wanna go up to my room? The guys will probably wanna watch the Cowboys lose to the Saints at three."

His room? Something seemed amiss. If he wanted to friend zone me he shouldn't invite me to his room, alone. I eyed him with suspicion, but accepted his offer.

"Sure, sounds good." I followed him up the stairs.

Walking behind him had been a bad idea. My eyes all but attached to his ass. His cheeks flexed in an entrancing rhythm with each step. I sucked in a deep breath at the top of the stairs, winded from not breathing the entire two story climb.

"You okay, Cat?" Jai turned around, dipping his head to look into my eyes.

Words stuck at the back of my throat, so I forced a nod. He pushed open the door to his room, holding it for me to go in first. I made sure to brush against him with the girls as I passed through.

"So." I spun around to face him once the door snapped shut behind him. "What do you propose we do now?" Pulling my arms behind my back, I stalked across the room toward him, making sure my breasts remained the main attraction.

His gaze zeroed in on the target. Pursing his lips, his Adam's apple bounced in his throat as he trailed up from my chest to look me in the eyes.

"I thought maybe we could just talk, get to know each other a little better." He gave a shrug and closed the distance between us even more.

The scent of his cologne hit my nose and spiraled heat

through my veins, straight to my core. There was nothing sexier than a guy who took pride in how he smelled. In fact, he stood so close in my personal bubble, I caught a whiff of his sporty soap as well. I closed my eyes, tilted my head, waiting for him to go in for the kill and sweep me into a delicious kiss.

I waited.

And waited.

Finally opening my eyes, I caught him across the room grabbing a black binder from his closet. A box tumbled over and comic books spilled out onto the floor. My eyes lit up like Christmas as I bolted across the room and dropped to my knees.

"Oh. My. God. What are these?" I picked up a copy of The Fantastic Four from 1961. Excitement rumbled in my belly as I brushed a fingertip over the protective plastic cover. "Is this what I think it is?"

"I dunno. What do you think it is?" With a tilt of his head, a smirk radiated on his face.

"The original 1961 Fantastic Four Limited Edition comic. Holy hell, it's signed!" I jumped up, clutching it to my chest. "It's signed by Stan Lee himself." Raising it back to eye level, I traced the signature of Stan's name with a fingertip.

"Wow. Then you'd be correct. I'm impressed." With a nod, his smirk turned into a genuine smile.

"I can't believe I'm even touching it." I forced back the tremors threatening my hands. "This is worth like thirty-thousand dollars, if not more with a signature. Not that you should sell it. Holy shit, please tell me you're not planning on selling it, are you?" I lunged at him and clutched the comic to my chest in a protective embrace.

He shook his head. "Hell no. That's my prized baby right there. I'd never get rid of it."

Letting out a sigh of relief, I gave one last look to the gold in my hand before putting it back on top of the entire box of old comics. An entire trove of geek treasure.

"You weren't lying when you said you liked comic books, were you?" His pursed lips accented his brooding brow. That smolder about set me ablaze.

"You thought I was lying?"

"Sometimes a chick will say a lot of things in the moment to get a guy to dig them. Just sayin'."

Brushing past me, his man nips rubbed along my arms as he took a seat on the bed. I spun around, forcing back a frustrated huff.

"You said that about football, too. I would've thought by now I proved you wrong."

"Yes. You have on a number of occasions." He patted the bed beside him. "Have a seat. I thought I'd show you some of my portfolios."

"Portfolios? Are you a model?" If he wasn't, he needed to be.

A laughed popped from his throat. "Negative. I'm far from a model. I'm the one behind the camera. My major is photojournalism."

"Oh, I dunno. I think you could do just as well in front of the camera as behind it." Goosebumps welled along his arm as I dragged a fingernail along his bicep. Forcing a straight face, I held back the smile bursting at the seams as he reacted to my touch.

I continued to work my fingertips along his tensed and twitching muscles until I reached the end of his fingers. His chest rose and fell in short bursts as he flipped the pages in his binder with his other hand.

"How about a massage?" I had to maintain physical contact. It appeared to be his kryptonite, I crawled behind him and pressed my fingers into his muscles, working my hands the length of his shoulders. The man had the tightest knots I'd ever felt. He either needed to readjust his computer chair or kick some stress out of his life. Each muscle twisted tighter than a pretzel.

"Wow, that feels amazing." His body swayed with my movements, and I finally worked through several of the larger knots.

Leaning forward, I pressed my lips to his ear. "Glad I could help."

"Um"—he cleared his throat and scooted almost off the edge of the bed—"what's your major?" The words came out in a slur between heavy breaths, and it took everything in me to hold back a giggle. I couldn't even tell what he said without seeing his lips or being able to discern the words.

I hated having to ask people to repeat things over and over. So I learned to lip read. But sitting behind him put me at a disadvantage.

"I'm sorry, what?" I asked and fought the embarrassment.

He turned toward me and locked onto my eyes. "Your major?"

"Oh. Audiology." Inching my way closer, I pressed my breast against his arm as I leaned in to view the pictures in his lap.

The stunning black and white photos distracted me. A collage of faces stared out from the pages. Such an array of emotions in one picture, it gutted me.

A young boy, of maybe three years old, clung to a barbed-wire fence, peeking his mournful eyes through as his mother's hand clung to him. My heart broke in two at the sorrow and despair on their faces. Another picture caught my eye of a homeless man sitting with legs out in front of him under a cardboard box eating a bowl of soup. Rain soaked and wilted the outer edges of his shelter, but the joy on his face as he spooned the soup to his lips said he was thankful for the hot meal. Pure, raw emotion lifted from the pages and ripped out my heart. They were incredible.

"Audiology?" He turned his head with a brow quirked, almost landing smack against my lips. "Wow, what made you choose that?"

I shook my head, startled from my thoughts. "Hmm? Oh, because I'm deaf." The words flew out of my mouth without even thinking. I froze like a deer-in-the-headlights.

Shit. I hadn't planned on telling him that.

CHAPTER 8

JAI

Her words hit me like a sledgehammer. Deaf? Holy shit! How did I possibly miss that she was deaf? *Damn, Jai, say something back to her, don't let her think you're an insensitive dick.*

"Um, I had no idea you were deaf." No matter how hard I tried not to, I stared at her like she was a two-headed alien. I couldn't think of anything better to say.

She dipped her head, hiding her eyes. "Most people don't. I hide it pretty well." She tucked long strands of chestnut hair behind her right ear. "See. Hearing aid. They've come a long way with cochlear devices. Depending on the severity of the hearing loss, you can get away from the clunky over the ear pieces. This one fits in to where you can barely notice it. And, I usually wear my hair down."

If I blinked and stared at her any more, I'd probably kick my own ass for being a douche. "Yeah. I mean, you talk perfectly fine. Don't deaf people normally have … like altered speech?" My thoughts tumbled out of my mouth less tactful than I'd hoped.

"I wasn't always deaf. It happened about ten years ago. A tornado ripped through my hometown. I suffered head trauma from flying debris as my folks and I tried to make it to the basement. At first it was just one ear, the side where I took the hardest hit. But eventually the other ear also suffered long term damage. I'm not totally deaf, but I can't hear anything but muffled echoes without them." Covering her ears with her hair, she slid back from me and closer to the edge of the bed.

My whole plan crashed down on me. Things went far differently in my head when I asked her to my room. I thought for sure she'd come on to me. Which she did. And I fully planned on halting her at every turn. Intimate life altering confessions hadn't been on the list.

"I'm … I'm sorry. I don't even know what to say." *Epic fail, Jai.*

She shrugged. "It's okay. If it weirds you out, I can leave." She crawled to the edge of the bed and stood up.

I grabbed her by the waist, easing her back to the bed next to me. "Why would I want you to leave?"

"I know it's awkward for some people." She bit her lip and took a hard swallow. "I can manage pretty well with the hearing aids. But sometimes I miss words here and there. Things get swallowed in the ambient noise. So, I learned to read lips to fill in the gaps. But if people don't look at me when they're talking I can't always catch things, and it's embarrassing when I have to make people repeat themselves."

"Why didn't you tell me sooner?" Every conversation we'd had to that point played back in my head, and I tried to remember if I'd ever made her feel uncomfortable. Regret gnawed at my gut.

"What, I'm supposed to say *Hi, I'm Cat and I'm deaf,* like I'm at an AA meeting?" Her face crinkled into the most adorable quizzical expression. I ached to kiss her even more.

I nodded. "Okay. Yeah, I see your point. I'm truly sorry. I had no clue."

Giving my shoulder a playful bump with her own, she flashed a sexy smile. "Stop apologizing. Please. I deal. It's okay."

Her hearing impairment didn't bother me as much as my awkward reaction to it. The complete shock of it threw me more than her actually being deaf. And I failed at conveying that without looking like a jerk.

"Well, what about you?" she asked.

Maybe I needed to pony-up, too. "I've always wanted to be

a photojournalist, hoping to capture things on film that words can't say. There's so many ways media skews things these days. Everything is subjective. To me, pictures are far more genuine than words can ever be." I tapped my fingers along the pictures wondering if she saw in their faces what I did.

"I believe you. These pictures are incredible. It's like I can feel their presence, their pain, their sorrow, the hope in their eyes." Placing her hand on mine, she ran a finger over each of the pictures. She undid me in every way, and I had to get a hold of myself.

Clearing my throat, I sucked in a deep breath. "I used to paint. But on my eleventh birthday, my father bought me a camera. Which was good, because I sucked at painting." I let out a laugh, hoping to change the sudden morose mood the afternoon had taken.

Her soft smile lit up the room. Warmth infiltrated the sadness that had filled her eyes for a few moments. "You're very good. At the photography, I mean. I haven't seen any of your paintings." She gave her own little laugh that sent a zing straight to my heart. I really liked the sound of it.

"Maybe someday. If you're a good girl." I tossed her a wink.

"I promise to be a very good girl." Her eyelids lowered, and her once sweet smile turned into a stalking panther grin. It lit my insides on fire. If she continued, I'd never get up from the bed, or I'd accidentally fling her off it with the massive boner tearing through my jeans.

The lump in my throat matched the size of my dick.

India. India. India.

Nothing like the life altering plans of your parents' outdated culture to rid yourself of an untimely erection. Just in case, I opened the binder even wider over my lap to cover the evidence.

Leaning over, she gasped into my ear and it shot adrenaline straight to my cock. So much for getting rid of it.

"What?" I managed to choke out.

"That picture, she's stunning. That smile. Is she ... is she your girlfriend or something?" Worry flooded her eyes as her brows pinched together. The honey coloring of them darkened, and her lips pursed to a straight line.

Was she jealous?

I traced the picture buried under the protective plastic with my fingertip. Yes, her smile was indeed brilliant. She always made me laugh. And I missed that. "No. It's my sister, Shree. On her wedding day two years ago in India."

A quick breath whooshed from Cat's lips, and a smile replaced the momentary icy stare. Relief? Interesting. But still, could just mean she'd have to start over with a new victim for her little project. Didn't mean she felt relief I wasn't actually dating anyone.

"What is she wearing? She's blinged out to the max. That ensemble is gorgeous." Cat tilted her head, leaning it slightly against my shoulder. The scent of her sweet shampoo hit my nose, and it took everything in my power not to sift my fingers through her hair.

Focus, Jai. Shit. How much more could I torture myself? Talk about Shree. Keep the conversation focused.

"It's called a lehenga. A typical Indian wedding lasts several days and the bride wears a different one each day. They go all out with the jewelry and adoration. We have an affinity for shiny objects and parties." A chuckle popped from my throat at the memories of my family.

"What's that brown stuff on her hands?" She leaned in and brushed her arms along my chest as she pointed to Shree's tattoos.

"Henna," I squeaked out, before clearing my throat.

"Is she still in India?" Cat turned her attention from the album to my eyes, and I locked gazes with her. My breathing stopped. I only noticed my lack of oxygen once the dizziness set in, and I sucked in a deep breath.

"Yes. It was an arranged marriage." The words came out like a robot. And I dreaded her next question, which I knew would come.

"They still do that?" Hitching a shoulder, she pulled away from me, taking her sweet perfumed self out of my personal bubble. And I wanted her back in it.

Giving a slight nod, I closed the book and tossed it on my desk. "Yup." I blew out a hard breath and closed my eyes.

"Are you going to have to do one? An arranged marriage, I mean." Her voice notched up an octave.

And there it went.

"Yup." I pressed my lids together even tighter, pinching my fingers over the bridge of my nose as I collapsed backward onto my pillow.

Wide eyes stared back at me as I reopened mine, and her color paled a bit. She looked like she'd seen a ghost. "You're kidding."

"Nope." Funny how I managed to lose every word in the English language, but the essentials of yes and no. Marriage, at least an arranged one not of my choosing, shut down my communication skills.

"I take it this isn't something you're looking forward to," she said, crawling along the bed until she reached my pillow.

I shook my head and blew out another breath. "No." Rolling my head, I looked up into her eyes. Gorgeous, and so full of actual concern it shocked me.

"Do you know who you're marrying?"

I stretched and grabbed the book back from the desk, flipping through the pages until I found the picture I was looking for. "Her."

Cat choked on another gasp of air.

"You okay?" I gave her a pat on the back.

With a nod, she cupped her hand over her mouth. "Yeah, swallowed wrong." She cleared her throat and sucked in another long breath. "She's gorgeous. Beyond gorgeous. She looks like she belongs on a movie poster or something. Who is she?"

"That's Kanti. Daughter of my dad's medical practice partner. We practically grew up together. We're more like brother and sister than possible lovers. I mean yeah, she's easy on the eyes, but I'm not even close to romantically interested in her."

The small fact that she dug vaginas just as much as me didn't help matters. She kissed a girl before I even did. But of course, Kanti's being a lesbian wouldn't stop the marriage. Because her parents didn't know. No one would ever know. A large part of India still had homosexuality punishable by law, making the mere subject of it taboo. Even though we lived here, the stigma of it in our culture followed.

"I'm sorry. There's no way out of it? I mean, surely if you don't want to marry someone you're not in love with, they can't force you. Can they?" She bit her lip.

I wanted to be the one biting it. Already plump and inviting, I pictured them kiss-swollen, aching for mine to be the ones that made them that way.

Shit, boner again. Dammit!

India. India. India.

Fuck, even that no longer worked. I sat there talking to Cat about my arranged marriage, and she still gave me a woodie.

"It's pretty much the custom in my family. There's a new wave of free thinkers in India and they're slowly moving toward modernization. But there's still some die-hard families that believe in the old way of life, my family being one of them." I gave a shrug.

"When?" She asked, her voice near a whisper. Sadness filled her eyes. Or maybe I wanted it to be sadness. But her face softened from the sexy stalking panther to one of sincerity and concern.

"This summer. After graduation, I'm going to India." The words tasted like acid on my tongue, and I barely choked them out. "My family and I are going over winter break to start the arrangements."

Silence deafened me. I rolled my head once more and caught Cat nibbling on her lip again, unconsciously clicking one of her fingernails lost in thought. About what, I wish I knew.

Inching her way next to me, she laid her head into the crook of my arm and shoulder. Without thinking, I nestled her against my chest, amazed at how perfectly my hand cradled the curve in her waist.

"I'm sorry." She slid the palm of her hand along my torso.

"For what? You didn't arrange the marriage." I didn't want this moment to end.

In fact, I ached to roll her over and punish her mouth with my tongue for bringing the subject up. And if we lay there any longer, I might have considered saying fuck it to Project Friend Zone.

The more I thought about it though, the more Project Friend Zone protected both of us from heartache in the end. I couldn't get involved with someone knowing full well I would have to end it by summer. Especially if I could get her to legitimately fall in love with me, and not just be part of her research paper.

Maybe we could just be bed buddies, once our papers got turned in.

And just how would knowing my predicament affect her paper now? Would she still go through with it? The more I thought about it, the more I became the perfect candidate. She could seduce me, and then dump me without a second thought, because I was now no threat of commitment. That thought certainly helped the boner situation diffuse, and my muscles tensed the more I thought about it.

"What's wrong?" She jerked back. "You tensed up."

"Nothin', just thinking about the stupid marriage thing." Clenching my teeth, I released my hand from her warm waist and placed both of them behind my head. She remained pitted against my shoulder and chest.

"I wish there was something I could do." She lifted her head to look me in the eyes. Soft fingertips slid along my cheek as she cupped my face. And dammit all to hell if that stiffy didn't just roar back to life. Sometimes I really hated having a penis. It inflated and deflated like a freaking blow up lawn ornament at Christmas.

For a brief second, I closed my eyes. But a knock on my door shot them back open. Mick ducked his head inside. "Yo, the guys want more kabobs. You game?"

I jumped off the bed, thankful for the interruption saving me from giving in to Cat's sly advances. "Yeah, I'll be down in a sec."

Cat huffed behind me, sitting on the bed and crossing her arms. I let out an internal snort and turned around with the sweetest smile I could muster. "You okay?"

"Perfect. Thanks." Scooting to the edge of the bed, the cutest little sigh puffed from her chest.

A part of me was happy she was upset. It meant our little game could continue. Because, truth be told, even though nothing could ever become of us, I didn't want it to end. I enjoyed just being around her, having something else to focus on rather than my parents disapproval of my career and impending sentence of marriage. She made things fun.

So now it was all or nothing. I planned on winning.

CHAPTER 9

CAT

"You hungry?" Jai asked.

Hungry? Seriously? It took everything in me not to throat punch Mick. I was so close to going in for the kill.

Maybe it was for the best. This afternoon took a turn for the unexpected, and fast. From me telling him about being deaf, to him revealing his arranged marriage; I probably needed alcohol more than I needed to nail him anyway.

Then the whole surprise stab of jealousy that all but bitch-slapped me. Where did that even come from? I mean, the dude was using me for a freaking term paper, why should I be upset he's unavailable?

Jealousy meant feelings. Feelings meant attachment. Attachment meant broken hearts.

Nope. Been there. Done that. Sacrificially burned the t-shirt. Jai was supposed to be a test subject, a research paper. There's not supposed to be feelings in a paper. Data and hard facts, yes. Emotions? No. Besides, even if there was something remotely there between us—a spark, some undeniable chemistry, he was freaking betrothed to someone. Not even going there.

Yet, he didn't seem the least bit happy about it. Maybe this was all me channeling his lack of enthusiasm for a forced marriage. Perhaps because it made him off limits, it gave me more of a challenge to go after him. Sometimes, I'm pretty fucked up.

No time to dwell on it at the moment. Regardless of feelings, or his attachment to the Indian version of Barbie, I still had a paper due and no time to find a replacement subject. Jai was it. At the end of it, he'd be off to India. Win-win for everyone.

"Sure, I'd like more of your meat." I mustered up the naughtiest smile I could.

Mick's eyes bugged out before he let out a loud snort.

Jai's cheeks flushed the color of pink champagne under the five o'clock shadow framing his square jawline. He was ridiculously handsome with a broody forehead and thick black brows. A pang of regret pinched my heart as I stared at his dreamy bedroom eyes, heavy lidded and so damn sexy. If he ever looked at me with them full of desire, my vagina would explode.

He pointed to Mick. "Your retorts are invalid."

Mick shot up both hands in defense. "I'm innocent. By the way, Cat, how's Angie? I sent her a couple messages to check on her, but haven't heard from her. She was pretty tore up last night."

"Um, she's okay I guess. Was sawing logs when I left this morning." This morning. Shit, I've been gone all day. I glanced at the clock above his desk. Five thirty. Outside Jai's window, the horizon swallowed the remnants of the sun, painting the sky in a brilliant pink and orange. "Crap! I've gotta run."

I grabbed my purse and shoes. I had thirty minutes to get back to my dorm in time for my date with WD on the computer.

"What about my meat?" Jai asked.

"Sorry. I've got something going on at six. Maybe, tomorrow? I'm done with classes at three." Squeezing between him and the door, my nipples grazed his taunt abs. The tingle zipping through them caught me off guard and a gasp hung in my throat.

"Six? Wait, what time is it?" Jai spun around and glanced at the clock. "Um, yeah. I gotta get these kabobs done, and then I have an assignment I need to take care of tonight, too. I've got class until five tomorrow, but if you want to come by for dinner, I'll save you some meat." He tossed me a toothpaste commercial smile and wink that almost dropped my panties.

It was a good thing I had to leave. If I stayed, I may go against my own rules and jump him like a horny monkey. What the hell was going on with me?

"Sounds like a date." I spun on my heel, but he caught me by the elbow and tugged me back, and I slammed up against his solid chest. My fingertips pressed along the ridges of his muscles outlined by his tight t-shirt.

"You want me to walk you or drive you back to your dorm?"

No way. I needed some cool down time, alone, in order to prep for my interlude with WD. The walk back to the dorms should douse the flames in my nethers, temporarily. "I'm fine. You should go tend to the guys before they make you clean the next party as punishment."

"Eh, they can wait. I don't like the idea of you walking alone. It's getting darker earlier now." His narrowed eyes held true concern, and it warmed my heart.

"I really appreciate it, Jai. But I'll be fine. It takes longer to drive there than to walk. I'll be home before dark. Promise." I crossed my heart, purposely dragging my fingertips over my breasts. And just as I'd hoped, his gaze followed the path.

He grabbed my phone sticking out of the front pocket of my purse and punched the contacts button. "Well, text me when you get there so I know you made it. If I don't hear from you by six, I'm coming to find you."

I bit my lip, forcing back the cheesy grin trying to push its way over my mouth. The sincerity in his voice, and almost demanding tone sent a wave of adrenaline through me.

I think he might actually care.

"Yes, sir." Pursing my lips into a playful pout, I gave him a salute and spun back on my heel before scampering down the stairs.

With a quick glance over my shoulder, I hit the last step and caught him giving me a salute right back. The nerd. It sent an internal giggle fluttering to my belly.

I all but sprinted across campus back to my dorm, making it in record time. Fifteen minutes to spare until my 'date' with WD. As I entered the room, Angie sat on the edge of her bed hugging a bottle of Gatorade.

"Where've you been all day?" She eyed me up and down before taking a long chug off her bottle like a pull of whiskey.

"Watching football with Jaidev." My internal giggles burst

from my chest as I flopped onto my bed.

"Who or what is a Jaidev? Wait, are you talking about that Bollywood babe?" Covering her mouth with her hand, wrinkles lined her forehead as she forced back what I assumed was the urge to let loose the Gatorade she'd just ingested.

My own stomach wretched at the thought. One of the very reasons I stopped getting blackout drunk anymore. No matter how much fun it was at the time, the morning after was a hell I didn't want to deal with. It got tiring using alcohol to try and impress a guy. I stuck to beer, my safety net where I knew my limitations.

"Yup. Watched the game, and then hung out in his room for a while."

"So, how's Operation Panties Be Gone or whatever you're calling it?"

"A little tougher than I thought it'd be. Turns out, he's doing the exact same project on me. Something called Friend Zone. I saw his paper on his desk last night. So, he's blocking me at every turn. But I'm bound and determined to win this." The more I thought about it, the more resolute I got. Maybe all that nice guy stuff was just to throw me off. But that look in his eyes, it told me so much more went on in his head than he let on.

"Fabulous. Let me know how that works out for you." She flopped backward onto her pillow. "I don't even remember how I got home last night"

"Mick apparently carried you in."

"He did?" She shot back up, then regretted it as she clutched her hand to her forehead.

"Yup. And he asked about you today. Said he sent you a message, but you hadn't responded so he wanted to make sure you were okay." I folded my arms and cocked a brow, giving her the sly stink-eye. "You guys hookin' up?"

She won the stink-eye challenge, only because hers were bloodshot. "Huh. Well, if I can manage to keep my head from falling off, I'll try and send him a message later. And no, we didn't hook up. Yet. If I didn't make a complete and total ass of myself."

"Well, the fact he asked about you says he's probably still interested." I gave a shrug and heaved myself off the bed. "I assume you'll be staying in tonight?"

"Yeah. Sorry if you wanted the room to yourself, but the slight fact that I'm dying makes it really inconvenient for me to leave right now." With a groan, she rolled over and pulled the covers over her head.

"Naw, I'm just going to be typing up some notes from today and talking to WD." Sliding into my computer chair, I flicked open my messenger and a blank document to try and put into words the events of the day with Jai.

"You're not gonna share your adventures from today with your bestie?" Angie mumbled from under the covers.

"Huh?" I spun around in my swivel chair. "You know I can't hear you mumble."

Angie rolled over and locked onto my face so I could read her lips. "Sorry. I want deets on your adventures."

"I didn't think you were up for girl-talk right now." Wasn't much to tell at this point anyway, other than things just got hella-confusing. Until I figured out how to stop him from making me complete mush around him, I wasn't about to let Angie know I could even be remotely falling for my test subject. I'd never hear the end of it.

"You're right. Fill me in tomorrow. Though I'll probably be a zombie, coming back from the dead. 'Cause I'm dying. Like right now. Dying. Dead." Another loud groan rumbled from under her covers.

"You need more Gatorade and your supposed secret cure?" I smirked and grabbed a new bottle of Gatorade from the fridge and her box o'pills from the vanity.

"Me love you long time." Tossing back the hangover-be-gone concoction which consisted of Vitamin B and Ibuprofen, she wormed her way back into her cocoon of misery and in minutes went back to sawing logs.

Six o'clock on the dot my messenger dinged, and my heart all but leaped out of my chest. I crashed back into my computer chair, pushed my glasses up on my nose, and clicked open the message box.

WD: Knock Knock

Me: Who's there?

WD: The correct answer would be WhoDat. Not Who's there.

Me: LOL Nice. So, how was your day?

WD: Complicated. Yours?

Me: Oddly, complicated as well. Why was yours complicated?

WD: Kind of a long story, and I'd rather not bore you with it. I'd rather hear about your day.

Me: Filled with football, food, and friends.

WD: Seems like it's missing another F word. How about some fun?

Me: I'd love some "fun" but my roomie's here for the night. So alas, I don't think fun will be on the agenda for tonight.

WD: Just as well, I wanted to let you know, that last night was kind of ... unexpected. And I hope you now don't think I'm some weird ass internet perv. I mean, I totally had "fun" and enjoyed it. But, it wasn't what I was after. Man, I really suck at this.

Me: No, I understand. I feel the same way. I don't want you to think I'm some internet tramp.

WD: You'll never be. You're my Impossible Girl.

Me: So, will I ever learn your real name, or get a picture?

WD: Hmm, I've got an idea. We'll do a photo reveal contest. The loser has to give their name first and take the other to dinner.

What could be so special about sending a pic? How the hell would I make a photo reveal special, shy of taking out a billboard.

Me: So, you're saying you want to meet me?

WD: Well, that would be nice. Or I could just have a pizza delivered to your dorm. LOL

Me: Ah, so you're already thinking you're going to lose the bet?

WD: Oh no, sweetie, I fully intend on winning this. I've got skills you haven't seen.

Me: LOL Oh, you think so, do you? Well, I just happen to be cultivating a plan of my own. So I wouldn't get all cocky. Unless ... of course ... your cock already is ...

WD: Impossible Girl! You're impossible! I thought we weren't going there tonight.

Me: We could ... I just can't really do anything about it.

WD: That's a damn shame. Because just seeing your name pop up gets me all kinds of cocky.

Me: It does?

My heart stuttered at the thought. And for the life of me, all I could picture was Jai, and I imagined what his cock would look like. Regret hit me like a sledgehammer. Could I really go through with this? Jai, sure. He deserved it, doing a paper on me. But WhoDat? He didn't deserve to be misled. The question running most rampant though, was I really leading *him* on or myself? Because the more this went on, the more I realized I had feelings for both of them.

WD: Mmm Hmm. But if we continue to talk about that, I'll end up paying attention to Rosie Palm and not you.

Me: LOL Well then, tell me more about you.

WD: Turnabout is fair play.

Shit. Well, we did need to get to know each other a little better than just our matching geekery. Hell we'd had cybersex before even having dinner or knowing each other's names. But something about the anonymity, the ability to just be a little wild and free had a thrill.

Me: Okay then. We each get questions.

WD: I'm down with that. Me first. What's your favorite color?

Me: Red.

WD: Mine's green.

Me: Duly noted. What's your favorite food?

WD: Anything Mexican. Since moving to Texas I've become addicted to Tex-Mex. I'm going to turn into a burrito.

Well, that screamed he's either really gassy or he likes things spicy.

Me: LOL I like seafood. My roomie's allergic to it. She can't even be around anyone who's had it. So I don't get it much anymore. I could eat my weight in crab and scallops.

And now he probably thinks I smell like tuna. Great, Cat. Why must I over-think everything?

WD: I'm now picturing you as a mermaid. With or

without a shell bra? Well, a mermaid was better than tuna.

Me: Definitely without. Shells seem like they'd be really uncomfortable.

WD: Help me with the mental picture, what color hair do you have?

Me: Chocolate brown. You?

WD: Mmmm, chocolate. Mine's really dark brown. In some light it looks black even. But when the sun hits it, there's brown tints.

Me: Tall, dark, and handsome?

WD: Tall and dark, yes. Handsome, well, I'll let you decide.

Me: Hmm, well I'm fun-sized. I'm only 5'4". Will I need a stool to kiss you?

WD: Nope, I'll always be there to lift you up. I'm 6'.

My heart melted a little. As much as I pushed away those butterflies, they fluttered back with a vengeance. But, one last test.

Me: Well, what if I'm not only fun-sized, but over-sized?

WD: I'll clear this up for you right now. I'm really not one of those guys that bases everything on looks. Yes, there has to be a physical attraction, but there are plenty of "over-sized" girls, as you put it, that I think are gorgeous. What if I am, too?

Me: Same here. Buff or Puff, I just want someone who can make me laugh, kiss my tears, and appreciate me for who I am.

WD: Are you taking applications?

Me: I need to see your resume.

WD: I'll work one up tonight.

Me: Good, you can send it with your photo. LOL

WD: Let's see, it's Sunday night. I'll give you a week. You've got until Saturday to come up with a photo reveal plan. Saturday night, it's on. You. Me. Eight o'clock. The photo war begins. Just you wait.

Me: I wish I didn't have to.

WD: Me either. But good things come to those who wait.

Me: And I bet your cum is good.

What in God's name made me type that? Regret hit me like a ton of bricks. I so wasn't this naughty. Like, ever. The power of hiding behind a screen name brought out a side of me even I didn't know I had.

WD: Impossible Girl being impossible again! Now I can't wait for that dinner. Definitely pizza, in your room. Because I fear that once I kiss you, I won't want to stop.

Oh, *you clever boy. Hit me where it hurts—the romance button.*

Me: Describe it.

Butterflies danced in my belly as I stared at the blinking cursor on my screen. He certainly seemed far too good to be true. *Please don't let him turn into some deranged stalker.*

WD: I'll show up with pizza in one hand, roses in the other. I'll toss the pizza on a table, the roses to the bed, and grab you by the waist. With my other hand, I'll slide it along your neck, up into your hair and cradle your head as I brush my lips against yours. Soft and sweet at first, until I break past your lips and sweep your mouth into the most delicious kiss you've ever had. I'll walk you backwards until you hit the wall, and I'll force your hands above your head as I make love to your mouth with my tongue.

Sweat beaded my forehead and my nipples could have cut glass they were so hard. Ugh, but I needed to stop picturing Jai when I read WD's words. I *had* to get WD's picture, and fast. The more I read WD's words and pictured Jai acting them out, the more confused and sexually frustrated I became.

Me: So, Sunday then?

WD: LOL I take it you approve?

Me: Yes. Dear God, yes.

WD: Well, I should end it on that note. I know you've got class tomorrow.

Me: Yeah. But now I'll have pleasant dreams.

WD: As will I. Goodnight, my Impossible Girl.

Me: Goodnight, Tall, Dark, and Handsome.

My heart sank as his name grayed out on the screen. I let out a soft sigh. Jai who?

CHAPTER 10

JAI

All through my classes, my mind spun everywhere but where it needed to be. Cat shook up my every thought, in between the ones riddled with stress over this stupid project I roped myself into and the impending marriage of doom. Not to mention I spent so much time on the computer last night my eyes crossed. By the end of the night, I somehow managed to wrangle myself a new photography project on top of everything else.

Sliding into my computer chair, I opened my inbox and hit refresh a half dozen times. No new messages. I glanced at my watch. Five o'clock. A ping of adrenaline let loose in my veins. Cat would be over shortly.

The computer dinged, and I just about leaped from my chair. My heart deflated as Kanti's name lit up on the screen.

Kanti: You there?

Me: Yup. What do you want?

Kanti: Okay, you need to get laid. You're awfully cranky lately.

Me: I can't believe you're even going there.

Kanti: What, just because we're stuck together doesn't mean you can't get you some on the side. I'm not giving up Maya. Why should you go without? I thought you were into some chick at school ... what's her name ... Cat? Your last thirty messages to me were all about her.

Me: I don't wanna talk about it.

Kanti: Yes, you do. Spill.

Me: I'm just really fucking confused. We'll leave it at that.

Kanti: You're less confused than you realize. You want her. End of story.

Me: It's complicated. She's using me for a paper.

Kanti: So are you. So hook up. You can still write a term paper as a result.

Me: How do you figure?

Kanti: Just because the end result isn't as you predicted, doesn't mean the paper doesn't contain viable research and data. Plus, you get some.

Me: Whatever. It's not that easy. You still coming to my birthday party or you ditching me for Maya?

Kanti: Of course I'll be there. But I'm going to try and sneak Maya along. If that's okay with you.

Me: Yeah, that's fine. Maya's cool.

Kanti: You know if there was a way out of this marriage I'd do it, right?

Me: I know. They can't find out about you. It's the perfect cover. And if it were anyone else, I would probably just move to South America and hide in the Andes. You're lucky I fucking love you.

Kanti: I am indeed. But my vagina will never be yours. So go find you one!

Me: Not happening. I won't put her through that.

Kanti: You're far too respectable for your own good. And that's why I love you right back. If only I loved your man meat.

Oh, my meat! I almost forgot I promised to cook for Cat again.

Me: I know. Say hi to Maya for me. I gotta go.

Kanti: See ya later.

I tore down the stairs, praying none of the guys had gotten into the butter chicken marinating in the fridge.

Score, it was still there. I tossed the pre-made naan into the oven to warm up and set the butter chicken in a pot. In minutes, a waft of butter, onions, garam masala, and cumin filled the kitchen. I loved that smell. Reminded me of my mother.

For a moment, I wondered if my mother would have even approved of Cat had the marriage to Kanti not been predestined. I knew she would have liked her, but getting the approval for a future together would be something entirely different. In the end, the whole thing just made those hard decisions simpler. There would be no future with Cat.

I put some basmati rice into the rice cooker and dashed back up to my room to change. None of the guys would admit it, but that rice cooker from my mom got the most use in this house. At one time they razzed the shit out of me for it. Then I started feeding them.

Throwing a white t-shirt on, I did a quick double check in the mirror as the doorbell rang. I chugged down the stairs as Mick let Cat in. Long chocolate-brown locks fell down her back like a waterfall as she shook her head, laughing at something Mick had said. Probably something about my domestic abilities.

Each sway of her curls revealed a glimpse of sexy bare shoulders. She turned and locked eyes with me as I hit the bottom step. The air in my lungs heaved into my throat and stuck there as my gaze drifted to the low cut V in her white sundress, accentuating two glorious tanned mounds. My shoe caught the edge of the rug at the bottom of the staircase, and before I could even say hi, my legs flew out from under me and I landed on top of Cat, on top of the sofa.

Damn distracting breasts!

"Hi," she squeaked out from under me.

"I'm *so,* so sorry." I peeled myself off her and dug into my pockets to just hand over my mancard. *Could I be any less suave?* "I'm just gonna go burn the fuck out of that rug. If you'll excuse me." I thumbed over my shoulder and dashed into the kitchen before my cheeks matched the color of her red lips.

I turned around, grabbing a couple of beers from the fridge, and she blocked the exit out of the kitchen.

"What smells so good?" She wandered to the stove and closed her eyes as she inhaled a deep breath.

"It's butter chicken. One of my mom's specialties." I lifted the lid, and her head brushed my cheek as she rocked to her tiptoes to peer into it. "Needs a stir." Pinning her between me and the stove, I reached around and placed a wooden spoon in the pot, giving it a slow twirl. My pelvis rubbed against her ass as she rocked back and forth to her tiptoes again to see. I wobbled as my eyes all but rolled into the back of my head. I had to pull away before I poked her with my kabob.

I handed her a beer. "Do you want a chilled glass?"

She let out a cute snort. "Please, I'm from Wisconsin. I've drunk beer from the bottle since birth."

I spooned our dinner onto a couple of plates and set them on the table. Strategically placing her on the opposite end from me.

"Oh. My. God." She covered her hand over her mouth as her eyes widened.

My heart dropped to my stomach. *Shit, did it suck?*

I hitched a shoulder, arching a brow. "Is it that bad?"

"No. It's amazing. Literally the best thing I've ever eaten.

You must feed me for the rest of my life." She sat straight up in the chair, hiding a blushing face with her hands.

A laugh popped from my throat, and I swished some chicken around in the rice on my plate. "Thanks. I really like to cook. My mom taught me everything I know."

"You close to your mom?"

"Yeah. I love my dad, don't get me wrong. But he's kind of a hardass. We've never seen eye to eye. We're two totally different types of people. Mom gets me more than he does." Well, until she went along with my dad and forced me into marriage.

"It's the reverse for me. Mom was the strict one. I'm a total daddy's girl."

"I kind of figured with your love of beer and football." I forced myself to look at her so she could read my lips, even though I didn't want to get sucked in by her eyes.

"Well, that mainly came from my brothers. But even my mom sort of watches football. In Wisconsin it's more of a religion than a sport."

I let out a laugh and shook my head. "My parents don't get into it. We lived in New Orleans for a while when we first moved to the states. So, really the Saints are my home team. But being in Texas, like you said, you kind of get sucked into being either a Texans fan or a Cowboys fan. I went the way of Houston versus Dallas."

Her face lit up. "Oh wow. I have a friend who's also from Louisiana. Somewhere. I don't think I ever asked him where. But he's a Saints fan, too. What made you guys move from London to New Orleans?"

I wondered just who this friend of hers was. She said *he* and my muscles stiffened. *Simmer down, Jai. She didn't actually say boyfriend.*

"My parents and Kanti's own a medical practice together. They started it in New Orleans, then built a satellite office in Houston. They bounce back and forth. I'm being groomed to take over the New Orleans location since my folks moved to Houston. We'll have the wedding in India, but we'll be living in NOLA." Just the thought of it made the butter chicken roll in my stomach.

"But I thought your major was photojournalism?" She sucked on the end of her fork like a Popsicle and I lost all coherent thought. Her piercing eyes caught me mid-stare.

"Umm, it is, but I'm minoring in business. They have another friend of theirs who will be the on-staff doctor, but I'll be running the office. I refused to go into medical and cut a deal with them that I'd at least do business and keep my photography as more of a hobby. They don't really know I actually majored in Photojournalism and minored in Business."

"Have your folks seen any of your pictures? They're magnificent. How can they doubt your ability? Why would they take you away from something you're a natural at?" She shook her head, dotted her lips with a napkin, and tossed it on her plate with a fury I hadn't encounter from her yet.

Was she upset for me? My heart twinged.

"You can't sustain a family going on the road taking pictures. They believe in a firm career that will support a family and keep you at home."

She threw her hands up and shook her head. "I can't believe you're just going to give up your dreams like that. My brain can't wrap around it."

I gave a shrug and grabbed her plate. Sadness clouded her doleful eyes. Cat had far more depth to her than I gave her credit for originally. Every moment I spent with her she surprised me.

We cleared the dishes together after dinner before heading up to my room. I closed the door behind me as she made herself at home on my bed. And hell if she didn't look perfect there. It sucked so bad how much I wanted to crawl next to her and kiss her until we had no air left in our lungs.

"So, I have a favor to ask." Propping her elbows behind her, she crossed her legs at her ankles. "Can you take some pics of me?"

Fuck yeah. Hopefully naked. "Um, sure. Right now?"

"No, I want to set up a real photo shoot. All professional looking. Would you help me? I mean, I'll pay you for your time."

I quirked a brow with a laugh. "You don't have to pay me. What are we talking though, like head shots or graduation type pics?"

"I'll bring the props, you just make me look good. It's a surprise for someone. Can we do it tomorrow?"

Make her look good? My skills could not improve on something already so gorgeous. I studied her, wondering what kind of ulterior motives may lie underneath this request. But, it would definitely add to my professional portfolio, so I was game.

"Okay." I crossed my arms and leaned against my bedroom door. "Oh, wait. I'm not going to be around tomorrow. I need to go take some pics for one of my classes that's due this week. Can we shoot on Wednesday?"

She nodded with a deflated smile. "Of course, that'll work."

"I'm done at four on Wednesdays. Where do you want to do it?"

"I dunno. I guess here? My dorm is much smaller than your bedroom."

"Here? In my room? You don't want to go outside somewhere? The light at sunset would make a pretty awesome background. I can picture the last rays of sunlight highlighting your hair. It would bring out your gorgeous eyes."

Aww shit, I just said that out loud didn't I? Way to out yourself, Jai.

She laid there staring at me, blinking, sucking on her bottom lip as a delicate pink blush colored her cheeks. And Private Peen tried to salute her.

Kanti. Marriage. Football. Dad. George W. Bush.

All the blood from my body shot straight to my dick, making the short walk to my bed an arduous task. A wave of dizziness nearly knocked me cold as I sat down, and my jeans cut off my circulation.

"Well, it's kind of a secret project and not for prying eyes. So, can we do it in here?" She shot to her knees and leaned against my back. Her hard nipples grazed my shoulder blade as she placed a hand along my neck. "Pretty please?"

"Okay," I choked out like a teen boy who'd just hit puberty.

"Thank you!" She leaned in and pressed warm lips against my cheek.

I closed my eyes and sucked in the scent of her perfume. A shiver ransacked my spine as her warm breath caressed my neck. The scrape of her fingernails along my arm did me in, and I sprung from the bed like a firecracker had gone off under my ass.

"Um, you're welcome. Do you like games?" I tossed her a

PlayStation controller from my desk and turned my game system on.

"Yeah, I kinda thought we were already playing one," she mumbled.

The dejection on her face made up for the underhanded move she just tried to pull. Friend Zoned—Nailed it.

Sliding back down on the bed, I bumped her over and she curled into a ball at the edge. "What are we playing?"

"I just got the latest Mortal Kombat. You up for the challenge?" Glancing at her from the corner of my eye, a wicked grin graced her lips.

"Wager?" Uncurling her legs, she scooted to the edge of the bed and stared me straight in the eyes.

"A gambler are we?"

"Let's make it interesting. If I win, the next game we play is my choice." Her teeth bit into the plump pout of her lower lip, resulting in a perfectly puckered pink mouth.

Nothing enticed me more than kiss-swollen lips. How she knew which buttons to push amazed me. And the lump at the back of my throat cut off all my oxygen.

"And if I win?" I asked with my very last breath.

"You can do whatever you want."

Oh, if only that were true. I'd switch majors like my dad wanted and play doctor. She leaned in and her remarkable doe-eyes just about made me jizz my pants. It was like looking at that stupid Puss n Boots cat. She had me hook, line, and sinker. If only she knew.

"Deal." I nodded and decided even if I had to resort to cheating, I had to win. Because if I didn't, she'd be naked and the Mortal Kombat term 'finish her' would hold an entirely new meaning.

Turned out my competition was a lot tougher than I thought. Was there anything this girl couldn't do? She drank beer. Subjected herself to vomit and stale beer to help me clean up. She liked football, comic books, and was royally kicking my ass at my favorite game.

Time to level up and resort to cheat codes. Giving her a quick bump to jolt her attention away from me, I thumbed in the quick code as she adjusted herself back on the edge of the bed.

"Oh. My. God. You did not just enter cheat codes, did you?" Climbing over my lap, she ripped the controller from my hand and held it above her head.

Soft, round breasts stared me down as she straddled my thighs. I reached up to grab the controller from her, but she shoved my shoulder and we toppled backward onto the bed. Both controllers crashed to the floor. A waterfall of molasses-colored hair shrouded me as I stared up into her eyes.

Her chest heaved above me, and my heart sped to a hum making me almost dizzy. I couldn't take it. Paper be damned. Sliding my hands along the sides of her face, I sifted my fingers through her silken hair and pulled her down to my lips. Just as the warmth of her breath hit my mouth, my phone vibrated in my pocket, and the theme from Star Wars rang out from my crotch.

Saved by George Lucas.

"Don't answer it," Cat said, pressing her lips against my ear. At that moment I would have paid for Jar Jar Binks to sing down my erection.

"I have to. The Star Wars theme is actually my mom. And she rarely calls, so something must be up." Sucking in a deep breath, I pulled my phone from my pocket but it had already gone to voicemail.

I slid out from under the little minx and sat up on the edge of the bed. My mother said she'd just bought my plane ticket to India, leaving a day earlier than we had originally planned. Meaning as soon as I took my last final, I'd be on a plane and spending my entire winter break over there planning a wedding I didn't want to have. Well that message worked better than Jar Jar Binks at shriveling my cock.

"It was about the wedding, wasn't it." She slid next to me and placed a hand on my leg.

"Yup. Mom just bought my plane ticket to India for over the break."

She wrapped me in a tight embrace, laying her head in the crook of my neck. Tender fingertips stroked the back of my head, threading through my hair. "I'm so sorry you have to go through with it."

Without thinking or caring, I pulled her closer, wrapping my arms around her tiny frame. The simple hug meant more than anything else. It was sincere. Neither of us plotting, scheming, or seducing. It was genuine. And I needed it.

She eased back from the embrace and cupped my face in her hands. "You know what? You need a beer and some Avengers." I tilted my head as I watched her grab a beer from my tiny fridge and click the TV on. "I've seen your t-shirt collection. I know you must own the DVD here somewhere." Rifling through my bookshelf, she thumbed through my movies until she found it. Damn, she had me pegged. "When I'm feeling down, only one thing can reel me in. Whedon."

Handing me the beer, she crawled her way onto the bed, and we snuggled up against the pillows to watch the movie. I rolled my head and shot her a smile. "Thanks."

"That's what friends are for."

"Indeed. Friends."

She tucked herself into that special spot against my chest, spooning her head into the crook of my shoulder. Her tiny hand splayed across my chest, and I fought with everything in me not to cover it with my own.

In moments, the sound of her deep breathing pulled my attention from the movie. She'd fallen asleep. I didn't have the heart to wake her. Instead, I just wanted to watch her. I clicked the TV off and readjusted on the bed so I could cover us up with the blankets. She stirred from her sleep, mumbling something and pulling at her ears.

"Cat, you okay?" I asked, wondering if something was wrong.

"Can't sleep with them in." Finally managing to pull out her hearing aids mid-sleep, she handed them to me to put on the nightstand.

Shaking my head, I chuckled at her sleepy lopsided smile. Dotting her head with my lips, I slunk next to her in the bed, and in moments was out myself.

CHAPTER 11

CAT

I kneaded fingers into my pillow, trying to make it softer. It remained solid, much to my dismay. Only when it stirred beneath me did I finally work my way out of my slumber. My eyes jolted open, blinded by the blast of sunlight aimed right at me through the slats in the blinds. Wait, my room didn't have blinds. I had curtains.

Where the hell was I?

Something thumped against my cheek. Rolling my head, I realized my pillow was a chest. Jai's chest. Adrenaline zinged through my veins, jolting me wide awake. His large arms enveloped my body, holding me tight to him. The safety of his warm embrace threatened to seduce me back to sleep.

Until the realization hit that it was Tuesday morning. And I had class at nine. I glanced up at the clock above his desk. Eight thirty. Shit, I had thirty minutes to get to my dorm, grab my books, change and make it to my pathophysiology class.

But his insanely hunky body blocked my path out of the bed. I'd have to straddle him to get over. And as much as I wanted to try it, I didn't have time, should he wake and things get awkward. Inching my way out of his arms, I managed to army crawl out from under him to the very far edge of the bed.

Lunging myself to the floor over his thick calves, in a leap that would have made the Olympic gymnastics team proud, I scrounged around his night stand and put in my hearing aids before dropping to the floor to find my shoes.

"You might want to brush your hair before you leave." His voice startled me, and I bumped my head on his desk as I jumped up from the floor.

Rubbing the now throbbing lump in my hair, I spun around and caught sight of him curled around a pillow with a lazy sleep-heavy smile, eyelids half-open. My lady bits shouted at me to crawl back in bed with him and spoon. He took sexy to a whole new level as my attention zeroed in on his fine ass sprawled across the bed.

I completely forgot what he said. "Huh?"

"Your hair seems to have a mind of its own in the morning." He pointed to the wild locks sprouting up all over my head. I glanced in his closet mirror and it took everything in my power to not run out of his room and never return.

"Let's never speak of this travesty again," I said, trying my best to plaster it back to my head.

He rolled out of bed, reaching for a brush on a nearby table. "It never happened." Giving me a wink, he ran the brush through my hair as I put my shoes on. With gentle but determined strokes, he worked out the last of the snarls until I could pass for human again.

"I'm sorry I fell asleep on you last night," I said with a wince, slipping my purse over my shoulder.

"I'm not." He froze as the words left his lips. "I mean, it's no big deal. I mean … it was nice."

"Yeah, it was." My lips twitched to a smile, and I dipped my head hoping the heat flooding my cheeks didn't blaze across my skin. "I wish I could stay, but I've got class in half an hour, and I have to run and grab my books."

"You want me to drive you?"

"Naw. By the time we got to the car, drove all the way around campus to my dorm and back, it'd be faster to just run. It's much shorter to cut through campus. But thanks."

He nodded. "So, do you have plans tonight?"

"I thought you had some pictures to take for a class?" Tilting my head, I eyed him with suspicion.

"I do, but you could come with me if you want."

"Really?" What kind of ploy was this? Friend zoning shouldn't include taking me out. He had to have some kind of ulterior motive. "What would we be doing?"

"Surprise." A wry grin slicked his face.

Bubbles of fear knotted my stomach. That sexy as hell smirk meant I probably walked right into a trap.

"Okay, I'll come pick you up around four."

Awkward silence surrounded us as we locked gazes. Do I hug him, kiss his cheek, or toss him a deuce? I had no idea what this thing between us turned into, if anything.

Nothing. It turned into nothing. I mean, the dude was about to get married in a few months. And he was still my research paper. But something more transpired between us. An odd friendship? Definitely some kind of connection. Maybe we could at least remain friends after his marriage. But how would his soon-to-be wife respond? She'd probably shiv me. I'd shiv me if I were her. Culturally, I had no idea how marriage or their customs on friendships worked.

He opened the door and stepped out of the way. I nodded and ducked past him, but spun around in the hallway and lunged at him in a hug. Lifting me from the ground, he held me suspended in his arms for a moment, tightening his grip around me. He released me back on the ground, and that sleepy smile curved over his lips.

"See ya." He smiled as he closed the door.

I indulged in a glorious shower after my last class, with fifteen minutes to spare before Jai came to pick me up. Tearing through my room, I grabbed my tightest pair of jeans and heaved myself backward on the bed in order to perform the shift and slither maneuver to get them on. My sheer black cropped shirt complemented nicely. A dash of makeup and a roll of the curling iron through my hair, I was ready to go as Jai knocked on the door.

"Hi." He glanced over my body like a hungry animal. Goosebumps shimmied up and down my arms as his eyes raked me over.

"Hi," I answered, doing the same back to him, taking in his beige long-sleeved shirt that hugged every muscle and jeans tighter than mine.

I grabbed a sweater and my purse and followed him out to the car, staring at his ass the entire way. It was going to be a really long night.

"So, where are we headed?" I asked as he pulled away.

"Well, first dinner." He glanced at me from the corner of his eye.

"Oh?" This turned into a date after all. "Where?"

"You're just full of questions." His sexy lopsided smile shot a tingle to my toes. "But I suppose I should ask, I was thinking seafood. Hope you're not allergic, are you?"

I blinked. This man walked right out of my fantasies. "No," I couldn't say fast enough. "Not at all. Seafood is my most favorite thing in the world."

"Awesome. I've been craving it. Tired of burgers and pizza."

I nodded and crossed my legs, hoping to keep my vadge from screaming at me. Any more sexy smirks and I'd need new panties.

"Then what's on the agenda?" I tilted my head.

"Have you ever been to the Congress Avenue bridge?"

"Nope. What's so special about a bridge?"

"You'll see." His sinister and seductive grin sent a wave of tingles through me. I could only imagine what was in store. But, this wasn't a real date. He's supposed to be friend-zoning me. Why the romantic dinner and a trip to a bridge? Unless he planned to push me off it. My stomach froze in a slosh of terror. No, there was no way he'd do something like that.?

We pulled up to a Seafood and Oyster Bar. My mouth watered at the very thought of it. As I reached for the door handle, Jai had already come around and opened it for me, escorting me from the car. Always the gentleman.

"Two," he said to the hostess, and she lead us to a little booth.

Dim yellow light filled the room with a romantic ambiance. Mulberry-colored booths lined the walls, and cherry-wood tables added to the dark depth of the room. Tiny glass globes held flickering votive candles, completing the mood.

And we showed up in jeans. Either he'd never been there before or he had a secret plan for the evening.

"Would you like a beverage?" The waitress presented their house wine.

I shook my head, but Jai had already given her permission to pour our glasses. All kinds of conniving thoughts ran through my brain at what he may be up to. Lowering the menu below my eyes, I stared at him, pursing my lips.

"Order whatever you want. My treat," he said, placing his menu down. "I'm totally going to gorge on oysters and coconut shrimp. While I love cooking, sometimes I just need a break. I'm the only one that cooks in the house, otherwise we'd starve, or be reduced to take out every night. Gets old."

"Why did you pick this place? I feel a little under-dressed."

"I wanted someplace quiet. I didn't want you to have to struggle to hear me."

My mouth tried to form words, but nothing came out. I did my best to smile and dove back behind the menu. I'd forgotten how pricey seafood was.

"I'll probably just do some scampi," I said, folding my menu.

"You sure? Their salmon is to die for. You should totally try it."

My mouth salivated at the thought of salmon. Oh hell, why not. He was just doing a paper on me, let him pick up the tab. I resolved to enjoy myself, despite the pretenses of the night.

He twirled his wine glass before taking a sip. Gorgeous kissable lips pressed against the glass, and I couldn't take my eyes off them. I desperately wanted to be that wine glass.

Cat, you're pathetic. Stop drooling.

I picked up mine and did an equally sexy twirl, sloshing some right onto my napkin in my lap. Raising it to my lips, I drained the glass in two point five seconds.

"Thirsty?" He chuckled and asked the waitress to refill my glass.

"Long day." I patted my lap hoping none of the wine made it to my jeans, or I'd have a whole new level of problems with a red wine stain between my legs.

"Well, let's talk about something more interesting then. Like hidden talents, or something that may shock me." He leaned forward on the table and stared me down.

"I thought I already did that when I told you I was deaf."

"Touché." He sat back, with a half-cocked smile. "But still, there's more to you than you let on. I dunno, I just picture you like commanding center stage somewhere. You have this air about you when you walk into a room. All eyes just lock onto you."

Sparks of adrenaline zipped through me at his words. He spent time thinking about me?

But a morose sadness pitted in my stomach. I hadn't thought about it in years as the memories flooded my head all at once. So many forgotten dreams. So many fallen tears.

"I've lost you, haven't I. What's going on in that pretty head of yours?" He took another sip of his wine as he continued a heated stare into my soul.

"It's just odd you say that. I mean, when I was younger I had this dream to be a dancer and singer. My folks put me in all kinds of dance classes and talent shows. I was really happy on stage." I dipped my head and took another long pull from the wine glass, trying to drink the memories away.

"I knew it." He sat back reveling in his being right. "So, why aren't you in drama here, or even music?"

"Because that all came to an end when I lost my hearing." I shrugged. "My equilibrium hasn't been the same since it happened. I now look like a drunk Muppet trying to dance. And without being able to hear, well you can imagine how I must sound trying to sing. Even once I got adjusted to life with hearing aides, it just wouldn't ever be the same. Anxiety pretty much became my arch-nemesis." I sucked in a long, deep breath and let it go with the thoughts of ever doing those things again.

"I'm so sorry. I didn't mean to make you relive a painful memory. I was trying to compliment you, but it went way wrong."

Remorse shrouded his dark-brown eyes.

"It's okay. Sometimes, no matter how hard you try, you can't outrun the things you fear the most."

"But aren't you the one who couldn't wrap her head around why I'd give up on my dreams?"

I pursed my lips and stared at him. He used my own damn words against me. The jerk. A cute jerk. But still. "It's different."

"Not really." He folded his arms.

"Okay. We're both stuck in a place where we can't really do what we want to. I get it." I slid a finger around my wine glass and stared into the deep purple liquid as if it were a Magic Eight Ball willing it to give me an answer.

Thankfully dinner arrived and I stuffed my mouth with food instead of ridiculously awkward conversation. Somehow, without even trying, we ended up in these deep, intimate talks. He knew more about me now than even Angie.

Project Panty Drop had morphed into group therapy.

CHAPTER 12

JAI

I understood now why arranged marriages stood the test of time. Because we men are fucking idiots and are less than tactful at precisely the right moment. Thus dooming us to be alone with porn and pizza the rest of our lives. Indians perfected a way out of that peril by arranging a marriage. It may not be love, but it ensured at least occasional sex and someone to talk to once in a while other than your dog.

"You know, they say oysters are an aphrodisiac," Cat said, and I choked on the one sliding down the back of my throat. She licked her fork like it was her last meal.

"Is that so?" I managed to say after dislodging the sex enhancer from my larynx. An aphrodisiac around Cat was the last thing I needed. "Oh, look at the time. We gotta go," I said, then actually looked at my watch. "We've got to make it to the bridge before sunset."

"Why? What happens at sunset?" She shoveled the rest of her salmon into her mouth and chugged down her wine like it was an Olympic sport.

"Magic." I paid our waitress and grabbed Cat's hand. "It'll be fun. I promise."

She eyed me like a mad scientist. We stopped at the car to

grab my camera, then walked a few blocks up to the bridge. I didn't have time to try and find a new place to park closer. I clicked off a bunch of pictures of the pre-dusk bridge area and the sea of people gathered on the sloping grassy hill beside it.

"What are all these people doing here? Everyone comes to just stare at a bridge?" The crinkle in her nose beckoned my finger to run the length of it. She didn't know how truly adorable she was.

"Just wait for it." I clicked off more pictures of the faces in the crowd blanketed by a pink and orange melting sky.

Children scampered around running and chasing each other with high-pitched squeals of laughter. I clicked a few pics of the happiness, proving the innocence of childhood, knowing that I'd probably not have any of my own. Kanti and I had never really discussed it. But since she'd never let me anywhere near her with my penis, I assumed it would be out of the question.

A ball of orange sat low in the sky, dipping behind a line of trees. The slight breeze picked up and rippled the water over Lady Bird Lake running under the bridge. As the horizon swallowed the last colors of the sun and gray replaced the light, a dark streak shot out from under the bridge. Then another zipped out and took flight into the sky behind it.

"What is that?" Cat pointed to the swarm of dark swooping objects lifting into the night sky.

I shot off so many pictures I barely heard her over the clicking. "That would be bats."

She froze, and a shiver shook her body from head to toe as she clamped her arms around me. "Bats?"

"Yup." I spun in a circle, Cat still attached to me, clicking my heart out at the sky and back down to the stream of people pointing toward the blanket of flying objects above them.

"You took me to see bats?" She punched me in the shoulder.

I hitched back and stared at her. "Yeah, isn't it cool?"

"They're bats! And they poop." Her sexy pursed lips wobbled as her attention drew upward at the undulating wave of flying rodents shooting out from the crevices beneath the bridge.

I clicked off several pictures of Cat without her even knowing it. The annoyance and anger on her face melted into awe and wonder watching the mysterious creatures of the night claim their sky. Gorgeous.

I shoved my camera at her. "You try. Tell me what you see."

She shook her head. "No, are you crazy? I don't wanna break it. I can't even use the camera on my phone."

"Just go on, try it." I folded my arms.

Her hands shook as she held it up to her face. I sneaked behind her and pressed my stomach to her back, holding her arms. "Here's how you focus." I twisted the lens, covering her tiny hands with my own. Her warmth bled through my skin and heated me from the inside out.

"Just push this?"

"Yup, whatever you see or you want to take a picture of."

Within seconds, she clicked off a few rounds and found her groove. The awe on her face as she captured the moments was even better than her seeing the bats. She finally saw what I did through the camera. Not a sea of people, but faces. Joy, excitement, awe, wonder, fear. Nothing captured the emotions like a raw uneclipsed picture.

I folded my arms across my chest, doing my best to hold back a smug smile. She spun on her heel and took several pictures of me. I threw my hands up. "No! Oh no. I'm never in front of the camera. I'm behind it."

"Not today you're not." She inched closer, continuing to click pics of me.

"No!" I turned and ran.

She ran just as fast after me, dodging people. I jerked to a stop as a mass of people flooded down the hill in their exodus as the last of the bats left for their nightly adventure. I whipped around and Cat clicked one final pic of my face before handing the camera back to me.

"You suck." I pursed my lips.

"Maybe one day you'll find out just how good." With a wink, she wandered down the hill, merging into the sea of people.

My mouth popped open as I watched her. Flipping through the pics she took, my heart stopped. Purple hued clouds hung above my head as I stared straight into the camera, one of the shots she snapped before I realized she was taking them of me.

The look on my face said it all. It always does. My eyes completely focused on Cat, and the depth of my focus and glint of happiness hit me like a rocket to my heart. I'd fallen for her. And the proof stared me in the face.

Shit.

I let out a hard breath as I followed her long brown hair getting swallowed in the masses. Jogging to catch up to her, I sifted through bodies until I got close enough to slip my hand in hers. She entwined our fingers and tugged me along behind her.

We walked in silence back to the car, still holding hands. She slid inside the passenger seat and grabbed the camera. The entire drive back she flipped through all the pics of the evening, a constant smile over her lips. That had to hurt after a while.

"So?" I asked, as we pulled up to her dorm hall.

She bit that sexy lip of hers and gave the camera back to me. "Okay. Fine." She threw her hands up. "You win. I had fun. With bats."

"You must learn to trust me, grasshoppa." Sliding my finger under her chin, I tilted her head to face me.

Shit, she probably thought I wanted a kiss. How the hell do I get out of this? But everything in me ached to kiss her. My body warred with my head as I leaned closer over the console, unable to stop myself.

"Well, you haven't led me astray so far." A blush hit her cheeks, evident even in the growing darkness. She pulled away and tucked her face.

Why not go in for the kill? She had to have known I was about to kiss her. She'd have her win. Her paper. Yet, she shied away.

She clutched the door handle and let out a sigh. I bolted from my door to get to hers, but she beat me to it. We collided against the grill of my car.

"Sorry," she said. "I should go. I've got some homework I still have to finish before tomorrow."

I nodded. "Okay. You still wanna do the photo shoot tomorrow?"

"Absolutely. I'll be by after class."

We stared at each other, neither of us really knowing what

to do next. Leaning down, I wrapped her in a tight hug. With hesitation, she eventually threw her arms around me and returned the embrace before darting up the walk to her dorm.

I leaned against my car and watched to make sure she got in safe. What the hell just happened to us? Did we cross some weird line now in our friendship? Not that we really had a friendship. It was a game. A dance. Some kind of weird war of pheromones. Yet, neither of us could deny we shared some kind of connection. Something unexplainable drew us together. And I hoped when all was said and done, we'd somehow manage to keep it. Even after I got married. I liked her, and if I couldn't have all of her, I hoped she'd at least still let me be a friend.

With a reluctant sigh, I drove home. As I parked the car, my phone launched into the Star Wars theme, startling me from my vicious circle. My mother.

"Hello?"

"Jaidev, this is mother," she said.

"Yes, I know. How are you, mother?"

"Did you get my message about the plane ticket?"

Dinner did a festive dance in my stomach at the thought. I prayed it stayed down in time for me to make it up to my room.

"Yes."

"Kanti's parents will meet us at the airport. They will be flying over with us."

"Fabulous."

"What is this tone in your voice, Jaidev? I am not liking it."

"Just tired, Mom."

"I do not know what is happening to you. For weeks now you haven't taken my calls and you disrespect me on the phone when you do."

"I'm sorry, Mother. I'm just stressed. I've got a large class load, trying to get everything in for graduation this year. And, you know how I feel about the wedding. I don't want to do it. I can't force myself to be happy about it. I understand the necessity of it. But I don't have to like it. So please, also respect me and don't make me feel even worse about someone else controlling my life."

"Jaidev, you know what we do is for your own good. We want you to be happy. Have an honorable and fruitful, healthy marriage. You have known Kanti all your life. At least we're not forcing you to marry a stranger, as I had to do. But look how your father and I turned out. It is a blessing. You do not see it now. But someday you will."

"You shouldn't be forcing me to marry anyone at all. That would be the blessing."

Bile singed my throat. Never in my life had I talked like that to my mother. Regret punched me in the gut immediately. "Listen, Mom. I'm sorry. I'm really sorry."

"Jaidev, they are only words. But please know, we love you and do have your best interest at heart."

"I know. Love you, Mom. I'll call you tomorrow."

I clicked 'end call' and slammed my car door. Nothing like ruining a perfectly good night with an impending doomed marriage to my gay best friend and a reprimand by my mother.

After stomping my way to my room, I flung myself on the bed. Part of me wanted to run back to Cat's dorm, take her in my arms and kiss the fuck out of her. Have one wild night of explosive sex, which I was pretty certain it would be with her. I wanted to just say fuck it to the marriage, to the paper, to my parents, and life in general. One night of something that I wanted, that's all I asked. Not something someone expected out of me.

But I wasn't hardwired that way. As much as I thought about ravaging her body, about having meaningless sex, it wasn't fair to her. In the end, not fair to me either. Because not only would it ruin her life, it would ruin mine, Kanti's, and my parents. It was like the entire world hinged on my love life. Or lack thereof.

As if I didn't have enough pressure trying to hide my career from my parents. I already succumbed to the shame of not following in my father's footsteps and becoming a doctor. I disappointed everyone around me on every level.

The one person I had a fresh start with was Cat. Maybe at least in her eyes I could be someone of meaning. Even if it only lasted a blink of an eye. I lunged out of bed and grabbed my paper, crumbled it into a ball and slam dunked it into the trash.

CHAPTER 13

CAT

Last night with Jai threw me for a loop. We had a really great time, and then he even went in for the kiss, and I froze. I blew the perfect opportunity to seize it, end the game, and write my paper. I could have had everything sewn up last night, and I failed.

The glimmer of happiness in his eyes when I saw the picture I took of him stabbed me in the heart. While I knew he was doing a paper on me, something in that photo said there was more to this than either of us had intended. And the fact that he was ready to give in and kiss me, giving his own paper up for me, I couldn't do it.

Plus, he was engaged. Whether he wanted to be or not, he was off limits. So, what the actual fuck was he doing trying to kiss me last night?

In a matter of seconds my remorse turned to fury. Did he think I'd just drop trou with him, let him have a pre-marital romp, then happily settle down with Indian Barbie? Wow, and for a moment I thought he was a decent guy. Ugh, the nerve!

Thankfully, I came to my senses and put Project Panty Drop back into action. That's it, the minute he attempts it again, bam. Project done. First, I'll smack his lips, then smack him upside the head.

I gathered my props for the photo shoot. Angie caught me on the way out the door.

"Back to the his bedroom?" Her sly grin meant I wouldn't hear the end of this.

"He's going to do a photo shoot for me. I'm planning on using the pics for the photo reveal bet with WD. Kill two birds with one stone."

"Mmm Hmm. So, how come you spent the night at Jai's then the other day? I've barely seen you in days."

"I fell asleep. It wasn't planned." Nothing with him had been planned, especially the falling for him part. It had really started to complicate things. Because the more I thought about this photo shoot, the more I wanted to call it off. I couldn't tease one guy with a boudoir photo shoot, only to give the pics to another guy. Just didn't seem right.

How the hell did I get myself wrapped up in this mess? I hadn't even talked to WD at all yesterday. Strangely enough, he hadn't sent me any messages either. We hadn't missed a day of talking to each other in months.

"Well, I think you're better off going with the guy who's here, than the guy who may be a perverted internet stalker."

"He's not a stalker. I know him. I've talked to him for a while now."

"You don't know his name or where he even lives, let alone seen a pic. He could look like Fat Bastard for all you know."

"There's more to a relationship than looks. That's part of what I'm trying to prove with this whole paper to begin with."

The more I tried to convince myself, the more I thought Angie may be right. Here I was so completely hot and aroused the moment I got in a room with Jai, and with each passing moment not talking to WD, that only increased. Out of sight, out of mind. An online relationship was definitely more work to keep the same fire with words that you have with chemistry in person.

Yet, Jai and I hadn't even kissed. I'd already technically had sex with WD. The whole situation seemed bizarre.

"Well, I'll see you over there later. Mick invited me to come hang out tonight. Some kind of game with a ball. Even thought I hate sports. But I figure, he's hot. Why not?" Angie gave a shrug and wandered into the bathroom.

"He seems like a decent guy. Try not to hurt this one?" I yelled over my shoulder.

"Hey!" She peeked her head from behind the door. "I can't help it if all the other guys were douche canoes. But I do admit, I kinda like this Mick guy. He was waiting for me this morning in the lobby and walked me to class. Since I hadn't messaged him back, he came to check on me. I never had a guy do that for me before. So, I figured I could sit through a game with him. We'll see what happens."

"Much better. Take advantage of it. You deserve someone who respects you. See you over there." I tugged the door shut behind me, juggling all the clothes and bags burying my arms.

I really should have waited for Angie to drive me over. I barely made it to Jai's house, collapsing on the step in a heap.

"Holy crap, what the hell did you bring?" Jai opened the door and helped scoop up the clothing littering his doorstep.

"Costume changes." I shoved the last of the bags into his arms and closed the door behind us.

Arching a brow, he shook his head and jogged up the stairs, like carrying all that shit was easy. Show off. I followed him to his room and helped him spread out the bags on his bed.

A plethora of camera equipment littered his desk. Next to it, he set up another table, tethering a cord from his camera to the laptop. As I pulled out the props, I took a hard swallow over the lump of nerves stuck at the back of my throat. *Project Panty Drop. Project Panty Drop.* As if repeating it would justify the stupidity of what I was about to do.

He eyed the bags then focused on me. "So, what do you have in mind?"

"I have a couple of clothing changes. I'd like to do them focused on everything but my face. Then at the end, one clear shot of all of me, including my face."

Folding his arms, hormone-inducing muscles bulged from under his tight black shirt. "What is this project for?"

"Top Secret. You game?" I bit my lip for full effect. I couldn't have him bail on me now.

He took a hard swallow. "Okay. I'll step out while you get changed."

I slid into the lacy black bra and panty set, wiping the sweat beading on my brow with each passing moment. Letting the hair loose from my ponytail, I shook it out and slid on the fedora. He knocked just as I strapped on the second stiletto.

I prayed I didn't pee myself when he opened the door.

Breathe. Just breathe.

"You ready?" he yelled from the other side.

"Yup," I squeaked out. As he opened the door, awkwardness oozed from my pores as I shifted from foot to foot, trying to figure out what to do with my hands.

Jai froze at the sight of me. Fumbling to get the door shut, he eyed me from head to toe and stumbled as he made his way to the desk to grab his camera.

"You have got to be kidding me." He closed his eyes and let out a hard breath before reopening them. "You didn't tell me this was a boudoir shoot." The camera shook in his hands, and his breathing sped to short bursts.

"Would you have still done it if I'd told you?" My heart hammered, and I almost succumbed to the wave of dizziness in my head.

For the first time since he walked back into the room, he locked onto my eyes. "Probably."

I tipped the hat low, covering my eyes and hopefully the blush raging across my cheeks. "So, where do you want me?"

He paused, and I could only imagine the things he said in his head. "Um, over there by that chair." I spun on my heel and stood next to an embroidered antique armchair.

"I borrowed a couple of props from the photography studio I thought we could use, not knowing what you had in mind." He fanned his arm toward the chair. "Okay, I'm not used to doing a canned photo shoot. I normally shoot raw, unposed images. So bear with me."

I nodded and took a hard swallow as his face disappeared behind the camera. Placing my hands on my hips, I spread my legs and stood in front of the chair. A bright flash hit my eyes and I wobbled backward, landing ass first into the seat.

"Holy crap, does that thing have any other setting than lightning bolt? I don't want to be deaf and blind." I rubbed my eyes.

His eyes shot wide open. "Sorry, I'm adjusting it to the room lighting. Give me a second." He snapped a few more clicks on the camera. "Better?"

"Much. Thanks." I stood up, and placed my hands back on my waist.

Lowering the camera, he made his way over to me. "You're way too tense. You need to loosen up a bit. It's showing in the pics. Look how unnatural that looks." He showed me the last pic and I could have passed for a femmebot. "You're not a statue. You're a sexy woman. Give it a little flair. Relax, have a little fun."

"Fun? I'm standing practically naked in your room while you take pics of me. I'm a little nervous here." Little was an understatement. I don't know what the hell I was thinking when I dreamed this idea up. It went far better in my head than the actual execution of it.

"How about a little music? Let loose, move around, just try and lose yourself in the beat and it'll give a more natural element to the pictures when you're not focused on me."

"But I have a hard time with music, I don't always hear it." I twisted one hand in the other.

His eyes softened. "Find the beat. You don't hear that; you feel it. In here … " He placed a hand across my heart, brushing heated fingertips across the lace barely covering my breast. Goosebumps erupted on my skin and he jerked his hand back.

I gave a nod, unable to form any audible sound.

He set up his iPod docking station and turned on the tunes.

"Strut." He demanded, and the driving beat of the music took me away from him and into another world.

He was right. The words may get lost, but the beat thumped in my veins. And I succumbed to it, letting myself go. I didn't just strut, but owned it.

The flashes of the camera disappeared as the music swallowed me. I morphed into the grown up version of me from when I used to perform as a kid. Good Lord, if my parents knew that all the money they spent on dance classes as a kid would end up benefiting me during a boudoir shoot they'd die.

"Spin."

I twirled around, holding the fedora to my head. Dizziness took hold of me, and I dropped back into the seat of the chair.

"Use the chair. Work it." His tone changed from soft, friendly Jai to forceful and demanding. It turned me on.

Kicking my legs into the air, I held the pose and covered my face with the hat. As the beat slowed, I hopped off the chair and rested one leg on it, tossing a glance over my shoulder back at him.

As he held the camera up, the hem of his shirt slid up his torso, revealing a patch of taut skin and the most enticing treasure trail I'd ever seen in my life. Everything in me ached to go exploring.

Time to up the ante. I stalked around the chair until my ass faced him, and I bent forward, gyrating my hips. Awkward silence followed, as the music stopped, but my butt kept moving.

He cleared his throat. "Um, maybe time for a clothing change. I got plenty of shots in this one."

"Okay, yeah. Good idea." I pointed him to the door. "Out."

"What, I've already seen you half naked." A sly grin laced his lips.

"Out." I pointed again to the door, forcing back my own sly grin.

"Fine." Shoulders slumped and lips puckered into a pout, he made his way out of the room.

I ran over to his closet and thumbed through his clothes until I found that white buttoned-down shirt he wore the first time I saw him in the bar. Sucking in a deep breath, I stripped out of the little bit of clothing I had on and into his white shirt, leaving the buttons open, except for one in the middle.

Blowing the breath back out, I opened the door, but hid behind it as he walked back in. He spun around looking for me, and after closing the door and sucking up the last of my pride, I turned around.

He collapsed onto the bed. "Holy. Shit. Is that my shirt?

I nodded, biting my lip.

"You're seriously trying to kill me, aren't you?"

"This is strictly professional."

"Mmm Hmm." He said, getting up from the bed and

grabbing his camera. "Okay. I have an idea for this one. Come here."

I closed the distance between us, and the scent of his cologne hit my nose, hardening my nipples on the spot. My hair brushed his chin as I passed him, and he maneuvered me in front of his window, opening the blinds just enough to let in the last of the sun's golden rays through the slats. But not enough that anyone could actually see in.

"Turn around and face the window. Open the shirt and let one corner fall off your shoulder. Keep it open with your arms out-stretched. I'm trying to catch the light diffusing through the white around your body."

I nodded and did as he said, and softer, more romantic music filled the room, and the clicks of the camera kept in beat. Just as the song came to an end, I eased my head around and looked back at him over my shoulder, letting my hair cover part of my face. He looked so handsome, legs apart in thigh hugging blue jeans. The tight black shirt was all but painted on his skin, and his muscles flexed as he held the camera.

If I had any panties on, they'd be soaked. I'd never felt sexier in my life. I wanted him. Bad. I had to end this, or I'd fling myself at him and ruin everything.

"That was unbelievably gorgeous. I can't wait to show it to you. You looked like an angel." He made his way over to me and slid his hands around me from behind, closing the shirt around me.

"Thanks," I said, eyeing his hands resting on my stomach.

Leaning forward, he pressed his lips to my ear. His heavy breathing sent a fire through me, plunging my heart into my stomach.

Oh, God, please just kiss me. Put me out of my misery before I become a puddle on this floor.

"Can I suggest a costume change?" he said right into my ear.

I nodded, brushing my hair against his lips. Taking my hand, he walked me to his closet and pulled out his black batman t-shirt and a pair of his boxers. "Put these on. And no hiking the shirt to your breasticles."

I quirked a brow. "You serious?" My heart hardened in my

stomach, and frustration boiled in my blood.

"Very." He left the room.

Pursing my lips, I did as he said and changed into the t-shirt and boxers just as he walked back in. This time without notice. Perhaps both of us got a little bolder during this experiment.

"Perfect. Just missing one thing." He rummaged through my purse.

"Hey!" I stalked across the room to him. "What're you doing?"

"Getting the last prop." He handed me my glasses.

"How … how did you even know I wear glasses? I've never worn them around you." My heart hammered into overdrive. What the hell was he doing?

"I saw them sticking out of your purse yesterday," he said, sliding on a pair of black rimmed glasses of his own. The square frames actually made him look even hotter, if that was even possible. I'd have to wash his boxers before giving them back to him.

"Turn around." He stepped back into alpha male Jai.

He grabbed a fist full of my hair, and my ovaries all but exploded. Tugging it into a tight ponytail, he spun me back around and my gaze landed on the expansion in his jeans. A boner the size of Texas just about split his pants.

"Now *that* is hot."

I shook my head. "I don't get it."

"You're trying too hard to look sexy, when you don't have to. If you want a sexy pic that shows just how hot you are and lets your true self come through, this is it." His warm hand held my chin firm in his fingertips. He stepped back and clicked off a picture.

Tears welled in my eyes, and the harder I forced them back, the quicker they fell over my cheeks. He won. That incredible, hot, perfect, asshat just won. Hook, line, and sinker, I was done for.

"I'm using you for a sociology paper." The words fell out of my mouth before I could stop them. Flooding with embarrassment, I brushed passed him to collect my things.

Tremors rumbled through every limb, and I shook trying to shove everything back into the bags. Heated tears continued to stream over my cheeks no matter how hard I tried to stop them.

"I know." Grabbing me by the crook of my elbow, he spun me around and handed me a thumb-drive of the pictures. "I've known for a while. Truth is, I'm doing one on you, too."

I gave a nod. "I know. I found out the night of the party. Which is why I can't do this anymore. It's just too much." He gave me every physical indication he found me attractive. But whether or not he was falling for me like I was for him, I had no idea. I just couldn't go through with it anymore.

Slinging my purse over my shoulder, I buried the rest of myself in the bags and fumbled for the door handle. "I'm tearing up the paper. I'm so very sorry."

"Cat, wait … " he said, running after me.

"Please don't. It's okay. I gotta go." I had to get out of there before my tears swallowed me whole. I just walked away from the man of my dreams. If I stayed and gave in to my feelings, there'd be no coming back knowing he was marrying someone else.

CHAPTER 14

JAI

I stood there watching my heart walk right out the door. The most perfect girl even my imagination couldn't have come up with just broke up with me. And we weren't even going out.

"Dude, everything okay?" Mick asked from the sofa.

Angie shot up from Mick's lap. "Did Cat just walk out?"

"Yeah, she had to go. I tried to go after her, but I think she just wants to be alone."

I should have gone after her anyway. But what they hell would I even say? I want to kiss you like nothing I've ever wanted in my life, but we can't be more than friends because I'm fucking marrying a lesbian? How do you even begin processing something like that?

"No, she doesn't want to be alone. She needs girl time. I should go." Angie grabbed her purse, just as her phone rang. "Cat, where are you? Want me to come pick you up?"

Mick and I stared at Angie. He mouthed *is everything okay* to me, and I shook my head. I mouthed back, *tell you later*. He gave me a nod.

"She's making me swear not to end our date early. Says she's fine. I told her I wouldn't be out late." Angie tossed her purse back to the floor and crawled back into Mick's lap.

"She make it back to the dorm okay?" I kicked my own ass internally for not walking her home at night. No matter what, I should have made sure she got there safe.

"Yeah, she's just gonna make it an early night," Angie said, before returning her attention back to Mick's lips.

Well, glad one of us would get some tonight. "Thanks. Maybe I'll try calling her tomorrow."

But neither of them heard me, so I made my way back up to my room. My white shirt lay in a wrinkled mess on my bed. I picked it up and held it to my face, inhaling a deep breath of Cat's perfume still lingering on it. A painful ache twisted my heart. I'd fallen for her. Big time. And I was the biggest dick in the world for not going after her and telling her how I felt. I owed her that much. Even if we couldn't be together, she should know it's not because I don't want to.

My phone buzzed in my pocket. I pulled it out and slid open the message.

Impossible Girl: Hey, you around?

I'd almost forgotten about IG. Hadn't talked to her in a couple days, which was kind of odd. We hadn't gone without at least saying hi since we started talking months ago.

Me: Yup. I'm here. Let me get my laptop up and running. Give me a sec.

I unplugged my computer from the camera. Cat's stunning pic standing in my batman shirt, boxers, and her hella-sexy glasses stared back at me. That's the girl I wanted. As incredibly sexy as she was in that lingerie, and downright fuckable in only my white button-down shirt, the girl I fell in love with was that geeky, perky girl in the batman shirt.

Then it hit me. I had to let IG go. For one, she had no clue about the impending marriage. Totally not fair to lead her on. I had no idea things would have taken such a turn in our friendship until that night a few days ago. But also, my heart belonged to Cat. Even though we didn't have a future, I didn't want one with anyone else but her.

It would suck balls hurting IG, but the sooner the better.

Me: Okay, I'm here. I'm kind of glad you messaged me. Well, I'm always glad you message me. But there's something I wanted to talk to you about.

IG: Me too. I had kind of a rough night. But it made me realize something, and I need to be fair to you.

My heart slunk to my stomach. While I'd been planning on scaling things back with her, the way this conversation seemed to be going she was going to do it for me. A pang of regret hit me. I didn't really want to lose both her and Cat in the same night.

Me: Okay.

IG: I really enjoy our conversations. You always know how to make me smile. And, under any other circumstance, I'd love nothing more than to see where things would go between us. But tonight I realized I'm in love with someone else. And, even though he and I can't ever be together, it's not fair for me to use you as second place when my heart longs for someone else.

Props for honesty. I agreed with her confession. It echoed mine. Yet, a stab of rejection still pricked my heart. If I could have rolled IG and Cat into one, I'd have the perfect woman. I might have even defied my father for that.

Me: I completely understand. I'm actually going through something pretty similar on my end. But why can't you be with this other guy? He'd be a complete and utter idiot to not be with you. Unless the asshat's gay, there's really no excuse.

IG: It's a long story, and part of it's my fault. It's so messed up. I don't even know where to begin to explain it. But, he's just the most amazing guy I've ever met ... sans you. Even if we could be together, I don't know how he really feels about me. And there's no point in finding out, since there's this huge obstacle between us.

Me: Seriously? What kind of obstacle could be that big?

IG: He's engaged to someone else.

Me: Wait ... what?

What douche would hit on a girl when he was already engaged to someone? Well shit, I practically did the same thing to Cat.

IG: Yeah. So anyway, that's where I'm at. I just wanted to honor our agreement. I owe you that much. And I hope, if there's some way you'll forgive me for leading you on, that maybe we can still remain friends.

Me: What do you mean, the pic exchange?

IG: Yeah. I had a friend take some pics of me. I planned to do a whole kind of stop motion video of the images. But in the end, he helped me see myself inside and out. So I'm sending you the best one that reflects who I am.

Me: Okay. I haven't done mine yet, though.

IG: That's okay. Maybe it's better I don't see it.

Me: Are you sure you still want me to see yours? You don't have to. I mean, I'd still love to put a face with your persona. Even if I never get a name, or know where you are.

IG: Yeah. I need the world to start seeing the real me, instead of this fake person I'm trying to hide behind. I need to embrace who I am. He made me see that tonight. So, I wanted to start with you, the only other person who really knows me from the inside.

Me: I'm honored. I really hate this asshole even more for hurting you like this. Just tell me who the douche is, and I'll take care of it. I wish I could at least wrap you up in a hug.

I really felt for the poor girl. How could anyone not choose her? Tonight really sucked balls all the way around. Nothing seemed to go right for anyone.

IG: He's not an asshole. It's not his fault. He's actually pretty wonderful, and you two would probably get along really well, come to think of it. He's adorably geeky and sexy rolled into one.

Me: Geeky I can handle. Sexy dudes really aren't my thing. I'm firmly team vagina.

IG: LOL Thanks for making me smile. I knew I could count on you.

Me: Anything for you. You're still my Impossible Girl.

IG: Ready?

Me: As I'll ever be.

IG: Geronimo!

I stared at the screen waiting for the file to transfer. All kinds of horrific images filled my head after that conversation. But, no matter what she looked like, she would always be my friend. And, I hoped I could still be hers.

Waiting for the file to open, I ran over to my mini fridge to grab a beer. As the pic came into view, my heart beat a wild rhythm I could have probably danced to, and my ass completely missed the chair trying to sit back down. All the oxygen in my lungs puffed out of me in a gasp as the pic I took of Cat in my batman shirt and boxers appeared on my screen. Tremors ripped through my hands, and my fingers shook as I tried to grip my mouse and heave myself back into my seat. Those gorgeous brown eyes hid behind her glasses, half covered by the sloppy ponytail I managed to put her hair in.

Fear froze me to my chair, once I managed to get myself back in it. All this time, I'd been talking to Cat. She just confessed she was in love with me … to me. Not knowing it was me. Holy shit. How was this possible? Did she have any clue it was me on the other end? From the tone of the conversation, it seemed like she had no idea.

Should I tell her the truth? I already hurt her once tonight. I couldn't give her a double whammy. A selfish part of me wanted to keep it hidden forever, knowing I'd probably never see her again in person. But I'd still have a part of her online as friends. I didn't want to lose all of her.

IG: Did it come through?

Shit, I forgot she was still sitting on the other end. Dead silence to a girl probably sent her into a tailspin of self-doubt.

Me: I'm sorry. I literally fell out of my chair. You're more beautiful than I even imagined.

IG: You don't have to exaggerate. I'm a big girl, I can handle it.

Me: Don't go down that road. When someone tells you you're beautiful, say thank you and believe it. Confidence is as much a turn on as beauty. Believe in yourself first, then you can believe it from others. So, is that "his" shirt and boxers?

IG: Yeah. Oh shit, I'm still wearing them! I ran out of his place in such a hurry I completely forgot to give him back his clothes. Probably a good thing though, let's just say I need to wash them before giving them back. He got me so turned on ... well never mind. You probably really don't wanna know.

I slapped my hands across my face, and leaned back in my chair, a little too hard and flailed as I toppled backwards onto the floor. If she only knew …

Me: He's truly a fool. As amazing as you look in them, I can assure you he'd probably prefer you keep them.

IG: Thank you.

Me: That's my Impossible Girl. I believe in you.

IG: I don't have any idea why I'm telling you this. I'm sorry to subject you to it. My roomie's out on a date. Normally she'd get the brunt of my random bursts of awkwardness.

Me: Actually, I think we leveled up in our friendship. I'm honored you feel you can talk to me about these things.

IG: I really appreciate you being so cool about this. You're such an amazing guy. And maybe one day we can meet. It's just not fair right now while my heart belongs to someone else.

Me: Trust me, I understand more than you'll ever know.

IG: So we're still friends?

Me: Always.

IG: I'm gonna shut down, there's a storm coming. Gonna turn in early. I'm not a fan of them.

Me: Sleep well, beautiful.

Her name grayed out on the screen. I spun around in my chair, hoping to counteract the wave of dizziness spinning in my head.

Holy. Shit.

After a series of several deep breaths, I managed to climb my way into my bed. Life was so unfair.

So. Unfair.

An hour later, I still laid there wide awake, just picturing her over and over in my mind. I even managed to resist the urge to get off thinking about her. She deserved better than to be used to get me off. Like it would demoralize her. Which blew me the hell away because I had no trouble doing it that first time in the shower. But now she was more than just a paper, or a project. She'd stolen my heart, and just the thought of someone jerking off to her, including me, sent a wild raging anger through me.

Like suddenly I had to protect her from all the evil shithead guys of the world. Including me, the one who broke her heart.

A loud crack of thunder shook me from my thoughts. Wind howled outside my window, followed by something pelting the glass. I sprung up from the bed and opened the blinds. Hail plunked off the house like white pennies. A flash of lightning so bright spider-webbed across a dark-green sky, illuminating half the city.

Mick burst into my room in a fury. "Dude, we gotta take cover. Tornado warning."

"Shit. For real?" I hobbled out the door after him, hopping into my sneakers. "Is Angie still here?"

"Yeah, why?" Mick quirked a brow.

"Because Cat's probably in her dorm asleep. If Angie's not there to wake her up, she won't hear the storm coming. She doesn't sleep with her hearing aids in. Shit."

"Hearing aids?" Mick hitched a shoulder. "Cat's deaf?"

"Yes." I shoved Mick aside and tore down the stairs.

"Where you going?" Mick yelled after me.

"To get Cat!" I shouted, as the howl of the wind drowned out my voice the minute I opened the door.

"Jai!" Angie cried out, running from the kitchen. "She won't hear you knock. Take my keys."

"Thanks," I said, gripping them tight until the pain surged through my fingers.

"No, thank you." Angie's eyes welled with tears. "I shouldn't have left her alone. I'm such a shitty friend. Thank you for going after her."

With a nod, I slammed the door shut behind me. No time for talking the hysterical friend out of the guilt trip. Kicking up speed, I tore across the campus dodging pellets of hail that pummeled my skin like rocks. I was pretty sure they'd leave a mark. I used to think paintball was bad. Raindrops the size of a Clydesdale smacked down against my skin. My clothes stuck to me, making it even harder to run. The wind slowed my pace as a huge gust slammed against my face, suffocating me with each step.

Shit just got real. What the hell was I thinking running out in the middle of a fucking tornado?

It was for Cat. I wasn't thinking. I was in love.

The normal ten minute jog turned into a twenty minute battle to get to her dorm. I burst through the glass doors, and ran through the halls full of screaming women.

Swimming like a salmon upstream, I dodged the horde of girls fleeing the building down the stairs. Limbs and breasts slammed into me at every turn. A shot rang through the building like a cannon. Blackness shrouded me like a blanket. Transistor must have blown. This threw a little kink in my plan. Crap. No power meant the elevator wouldn't be working. Had to find the stairs.

By the time I hit the third floor breathing became a chore. I stopped to suck in a huge breath, bracing my hands on my knees.

Three twelve. Three twelve. I ran my fingertips over each door in the dark trying to feel the numbers. Three twenty. Shit, they were going up. Wrong way. I spun around and ran back down the opposite hall. Three fourteen. Three twelve. Found it.

My hands shook like a meth addict as I fumbled with the

keys. No time for fear. I burst through the door.

"Cat!" I yelled her name without thinking. Maybe a part of me hoped she'd had her hearing aids in and she'd gotten out.

"Cat!" I shouted again as I tripped over a chair in the dark. Having never been further than her front door, I had no idea the layout and pretty much caught every piece of furniture they had with my foot. I would really suck at being blind.

Golf ball sized hail rained down outside the window, illuminated by a lightning streak from Zeus himself. But it allowed me to get a quick look at the room, and I found Cat asleep in her bed in the corner.

I dashed over to her, trying to think of a way to wake her up without freaking her shit out. Nothing came to mind, and I had no time for anything other than a less than romantic shakedown.

"Cat." I dropped to my knees at the side of her bed, giving her shoulders a shake.

Her eyes fluttered open before jolting as wide as saucers and a scream burst from her lips. It blew me back, and I landed on my ass. Damn, she channeled her inner Black Canary Cry.

I crawled my way back to her, but she flung herself out of the bed and reached for the lamp, trying with desperation to get it to turn on.

"The power is out," I shouted, hoping maybe she could hear something in the muffled echoes that would tell her it's my voice. "Storm. Must get you out."

"My hearing aids," she mumbled, patting her hand on the nightstand.

I dove to the table and helped her try to locate them. My fingertips slipped against something plastic, sending them crashing to the floor. Cat plunged to her knees, patting the ground in front of her. I slid my hands on either side of her face, and locked eyes with her. A streak of lightning blazed outside the window, followed by an ear-splitting crash of thunder. But in that moment I was thankful for the lightning. She saw my face.

Wide eyes stared back at me, filled with relief then fear. Her warm arms slid around my neck as she flung herself against my chest. With one hand, I continued to pat the floor looking for her hearing aids. The other held her tight against my body. Clutching the little plastic devices in my fingers, I handed them back to her.

She slipped them into her ears. Another loud burst of thunder hit, this time shaking the building. Slamming her hands against her ears, she buried her head against my chest. "What's happening?"

"There's a bad storm. Possibly a tornado. I came to get you out of here. We have to get to the lowest level of the building. It's not safe this high up." I grabbed her hand, but she refused to budge.

Trembling hands clung to the sides of her head as she rocked back and forth in my lap. "No. Not again. That noise. Not again."

I shook my head trying to make sense of what she was saying. "What noise? What's wrong, Cat?"

Then I heard it too. That unmistakable sound like a roaring train. Howling winds hammered the windows with debris. Tremors ravaged my body, but they weren't from my muscles or even Cat's. The building shook like a baby rattle, with us inside it.

"I can't do this. I can't go through this again. Not again." A flash of lightning blinded us, and the last thing that burned into my mind was the fear on Cat's tear-soaked face.

A shower of glass rained down on top of us before I ever heard the crash. We dove to the floor, and I threw myself on top of her. Baseballs of hail blew through the windows, and debris mixed with shattered glass battered us. Shards of it impaled my skin like tiny daggers, sending spikes of pain up and down my back.

It hit me then what Cat had been mumbling. She lost her hearing as a result of a head injury in a tornado. She had to relive it all over again. Searing pain ravaged my back as I tried to push myself up from the floor. I had to get us out of there. Or at least to the bathroom. We needed to get as far away from the windows as possible.

Adrenaline surged through my veins as I scooped Cat from the floor. I carried her to the bathroom and laid her in the tub. Running back into the room, I scrounged around for some pillows and ripped a blanket from Angie's bed, not covered in glass. I tucked the pillow under Cat's head and climbed in on top of her, covering us both with the blanket.

Her body trembled beneath me, and I did my best to cradle her as tight against my chest as I could manage in the tiny bathtub. For such a small person, she about squeezed the air from my lungs. Full on panic-attack mode set in. I had to get her calmed down.

"Cat, sweetie, look at me. Look at my face." Only occasional bursts of lightning lit up the pitch-black bathroom. But I slid my hands against her cheeks and pressed my forehead to hers letting her know I was still there. "We're going to be okay. I promise you, I'll keep you safe."

"I'm so scared, Jai." Her trembling lips brushed against mine in the dark. Swiping at the tears raining down her face, I tilted her head and pulled her bottom lip between mine. Fear pitched and rolled in my stomach. From the storm, or because I kissed Cat, I didn't know.

I eased away from her lips, only to have her swipe back at them with her mouth, pulling me into a full-on kiss. In that moment, I didn't care about anything. Not the storm. Not the wedding. Not my father.

Only Cat.

Our mouths melted together, and our tongues tangled with a fury I'd never known. Cradling my head with her arms, she pressed herself harder against me, and I held onto her for dear life. Like she tethered us to the Earth, together. My fingertips curled into her shirt … my shirt. She was still wearing my clothes.

Her fingers explored my skin in the dark, sending heated pulses all over my body. Part of me thought it was all some dream. I couldn't really be kissing Cat. In a bathtub. In the middle of a tornado.

But her soft moan tingled against my lips as she deepened the kiss, and I claimed her. Even if it was just one single moment in time, I put everything I could into that kiss. Everything that had been bottled up inside me melted away with each swipe of our tongues. I kissed her until all the air left my lungs.

Cat pulled back, lingering on my bottom lip. Without thinking, I gripped tighter to her shirt, not wanting her to pull away. We sat in the dark, our lips barely touching, just knowing the other was right there. She curled her fingers around my hand, and I gripped her tight.

"I don't hear it anymore," she said. Her warm breath tickled my wet lips.

"You think it's over?" I released my death grip on her, and pushed myself up and out of the tub. Feeling for her hand, I pulled her up alongside me and helped her step out.

I clutched tight to her waist and held her next to me as we made our way from the bathroom into the bedroom. Intermittent flashes of lightning blinked across the sky in the distance.

Chunks of glass crunched under my feet. I spun around and swung Cat into my arms, sitting her down in one of the many chairs I tripped over on my way in. "There's glass everywhere and you don't have any shoes on. Stay put. Where are your sneakers?"

"In my closet, on the bottom right-hand side." I walked to the closet, but stopped short when she refused to let my hand go.

"It's okay. We're still alive. But we need to get out of here. I have no idea if the building is stable. It could collapse." Pulling her hand to my lips, I dotted it with a quick kiss and dashed to her closet to grab her shoes. After slipping them on her feet, I helped her out of the chair.

With each step, the floor creaked and crunched beneath our weight. She launched herself against my chest, and I wrapped my arms around her as we made our way to the hallway. What was left of it. A gaping hole greeted us at the other end. My heart plunged to my stomach and hammered there. I fought the panic-inducing nausea, forcing myself to keep it together for Cat.

I had just walked the length of that hallway in my rush to get to her. To know the very floor I walked on only moments ago was no longer there freaked my shit out. I wished I could have covered Cat's eyes so she didn't have to see it. She still shivered against my body.

How the hell would we get out of there? The stairwell I climbed to get up to her floor no longer existed.

"Oh, God." Cat clasped a hand to her mouth and buried her face against me.

I stroked the back of her head and placed a soft kiss into her hair. "Hey, we're going to be okay. I've got you."

"What about all the other girls? What if someone's hurt?" The panic in her voice matched the fear in her eyes as she looked up at me. "Do you hear anyone?"

I shook my head. "I think the majority of them got to safety. They all rushed out as I ran in to get you."

"Why? Why would you do that?" She shook her head, launched a punch at my shoulder, and collapsed against me in a burst of tears. "You could've gotten killed. For me!"

"I did it for that very reason." I cradled my hands along her cheeks and made her look in my eyes. "Because I couldn't let anything happen to *you*."

"You're insane. You risked your life for me." Confusion darkened her eyes. Like she couldn't understand that I really had feelings for her. She had no idea I'd do it again in a heartbeat.

I brushed a tear away with my thumb. "I didn't even think about it. I just did it. Let's just relish the fact that we're both still alive. We can argue about my insanity later, when we're not in a building that's about to collapse."

With a nod, Cat brushed one last tear slipping over her cheek. "There's a staircase around the back corner. Let's see if that one is still there."

We clasped hands and walked to the staircase. Feeling our way in the pitch-dark, we each pressed a hand to the wall and made a slow, calculated decent down the stairs.

I opened the bottom door to a state of complete chaos. Sirens blared in the distance, followed by brilliant flashing red and blue lights. Droves of people gathered around the campus, shock covering their faces as they took in the surroundings. The wails of sobbing girls surrounded us as Cat's dorm-mates looked at what remained of their living quarters.

I glanced at Cat as she stood emotionless at the sight. She brushed away a tear slicking her trembling lips. Slipping my arms around her from behind, I tucked her against me. Nothing I could say or do in that moment would be enough. She just needed to be held. To know she wasn't alone. And to be reassured she had once again survived.

CHAPTER 15

CAT

Flashing lights, sirens, and screams swirled in the air around me. I should have turned my hearing aids off. Too many memories. Too many feelings. I didn't know what I would have done if Jai hadn't come to get me.

Died? Perhaps.

Injured? More than likely.

I stared at him as he sat inside an ambulance. His back took the brunt of the shattered window. Though from what the paramedics said, he was lucky none of the cuts were very deep. Mainly surface scrapes.

That insane guy ran across campus in the middle of a tornado to make sure I was okay. Every emotion welled up in me at once and lodged itself in the back of my throat. Just when I thought I couldn't cry anymore, the tears flooded me again.

"Cat!" Angie shouted from behind me. I spun around and fell into her arms. "Oh. My. God. What the hell happened?"

My teeth chattered together as I struggled to keep the tears from crashing over my cheeks at the thought of having to relive it again in words. "Um … it's all kind of a blur. Jai … he..." I sniffed back the onslaught of tears as Angie ran her hands up and down my arms.

"It's okay, hun. You don't have to talk about it. It's over now." Her warm hug helped, but didn't make me feel safe like Jai's did. All through the storm, only his protective embrace got me through. And that kiss. That incredible breath-taking kiss.

Who kisses in the middle of a tornado?

Maybe for a moment he thought we were going to die. There was a point in there I thought we would, too.

Mick made his way over to us and tapped Angie on the shoulder. "They say the building's not safe. They have to check it out before they'll let anyone inside to get their things. Probably won't be until tomorrow or the day after. Classes have been canceled for the rest of the week."

A large, warm hand slid along my waist from behind. I knew without even turning around it was Jai. The curve of his arm held tight to my body, and I leaned back against his chest.

"You guys okay?" Jai asked.

Mick gave a nod and clutched Angie's hand. "Yeah, we all made it to the bathroom in time. The house is fine. Bottom window in the living room blew out. But other than that, it didn't take any damage. They said it was a possible EF-2 that hit the north side of campus."

Jai nodded and rested his chin on the top of my head. "The girls should stay with us tonight, until they can make other arrangements for another dorm. From the looks of it, it'll be a while before they'll be moving back in."

We all glanced to my dorm, well what was left of it. Seeing it now from the outside gutted me. An entire wall on the north side had been blown away. Bricks littered the ground, buried between uprooted trees, clothing, desks, twisted up street lamps, and a few cars that had seen better days. We survived because my room happened to be on the south end of the building, the only side with a wall still standing.

"Let's head back to the house. We're all exhausted." Jai nudged me forward, before clasping his hand over mine.

Silence dominated our walk back. Only the odd rumble of now distant thunder and a few lingering sirens echoed. Jai swept his thumb in gentle strokes along my hand as we walked. I had no idea what any of it meant. The kiss. The way he held me. Our holding hands.

They say traumatic situations bring people together. But we couldn't be together. Nothing but confusion and pain could come of it.

"Let's get you cleaned up. I'll give you a new shirt and another pair of boxers. Tomorrow, since we don't have any classes, I'll take you to the store to get some temporary clothes." He brushed a hand through my hair, but jerked it back out. "Shit. You've got shards of glass all in your hair."

I ran a hand through my locks and a piece of one pricked my fingertip. "Ugh."

He pulled my finger to his mouth, pressing his lips in a gentle kiss against my skin. "I'll help you get it out. I may need the return favor. I'm sure there's some in mine, too. We can sit in *my* bathtub this time and pick glass out of each other's hair like a couple of monkeys."

I snorted. "Nothing says sexy like picking debris out of each other's hair."

He grabbed a change of clothes for each of us, then walked me to the bathroom. I sat on the toilet while he combed through my hair for debris.

"I think I got it all. But let me wash your hair, just in case." He turned on the shower head and panic riddled my heart.

I held a hand up. "You don't have to wash my hair. I can manage a shower."

"Yes, I'm sure you're a big girl now and can shower on your own." He laughed. "But you can't see if there's a piece of glass I missed. And I don't want you slicing your hand open washing your hair. So, get in there." Soft creases lined the outer edges of his narrowed eyes. They said there would be no arguing.

"All I've got is Suave. It'll have to do for now. We'll pick up some toiletries for you as well tomorrow. I'm afraid I don't stock up on chick stuff much."

I forced back the smile curling over my lips. A flutter happy-danced in my belly. That meant he didn't have a parade of women spending time over night at his place. Well, not that many would, seeing as how he was soon-to-be-hitched.

I took out my hearing aids and placed them on the counter.

Jai slid his hands along my cheeks and tilted my head to face him. "Can you read my lips?"

I gave a nod, and he stroked his thumb along my cheeks before I stepped into the shower, fully clothed, and let him run the water through my hair. Suds streaked my face, dripping into my eyes. I swiped at them in a fury.

"Shit, sorry. This is why I'm in photography, and not beauty school." He looked around. "And, I failed to bring towels." He stripped out of his shirt and slid it down my face, wiping away the soap from my eyes. "Did I get it all?"

I nodded. The room spun around me as I stared at his bare chest. My legs wobbled, and I sucked in a gasp of air realizing I'd stopped breathing.

"Whoa. Careful," he said, rinsing the last of the soap from my hair.

Jello. My body turned to complete Jello, and I slammed my hand against the wall just trying to remain upright.

"You okay?" He jumped into the shower with me, catching my slipping body in his arms.

"No," I choked out, gripping to his arms for dear life. My soaking wet shirt did little to hide my rock hard nipples as they scraped against his chest. Then all dignity left me as his boxers, weighted down with water, slid right off my hips and swallowed my ankles.

A laugh popped from his throat as we both looked down at the thud in the bottom of the tub.

I traced the edge of his drenched jeans, and my fingertip slid along his waist. Shivering beneath my touch, he tensed his stomach, and a ridge of muscles rippled down his torso. Suddenly I was soaked too, and not from the water.

"We shouldn't do this … I mean … we can't." Heavy breaths heaved from his chest as he reached behind me to shut the water off. For a moment my head pressed against his bare chest and my cheek soaked in his warmth.

I nodded, regret and relief taking equal punches at my heart.

Leaning against his body, he helped me from the tub and I slipped my hearing aids back in. "I've got towels in my room. Let's get you out of what's left of your wet clothes."

Grabbing my hand, we trotted across the hall to his room. He took a couple of towels from his closet and wrapped one around me. Shudders ravaged my body, and I succumbed to the tremors.

"You're shivering." He swallowed hard as he closed his eyes, and reached for the hem of my shirt. "We have to get you out of this." Time slowed as his hands grazed my stomach, pulling the shirt up my body and over my head.

Opening his eyes, he locked onto my gaze. "Everything about this is so wrong. But I've never wanted anything more in my entire life than to take you, right here. Right now."

I nibbled on my trembling lip and dropped the towel to the floor. "One night. Just one night."

His jaw tightened. Clenching his hands at his side, his gaze raked over my body from head to toe until he locked back onto my eyes. "You don't understand, Cat. I don't want just one night with you."

"I get it. I'm sorry." Nodding, I dropped to a squat and picked the towel up. "Just answer me one thing. Why did you come after me tonight?"

"I'd think that was pretty obvious."

I shook my head and wrapped the towel around me again. Jai grabbed my wrist with one hand and ripped the towel off with the other. Both hands fisted in my wet hair as he pulled me to him and crushed his mouth over mine.

A shocked moan rumbled in my throat as our tongues slid in a sensual dance. Tears slipped over my cheeks as I wrapped my arms around his neck and kissed him back with everything in me. Just one night.

His hands traveled down my body to my waist, and he picked me up. I wrapped my legs around his hips and he carried me across the room, easing me onto his bed. He broke the kiss, and I sucked in a deep breath as I shoved his jeans over his hips and he worked himself out of them.

With long, lithe movements, he crawled over me like a stalking panther. I lunged up at him and yanked him down on top of me in need of his kiss. Everything in my body raged as if it were on fire. One hand cupped the back of my head, kissing me as if his life depended on it. His other hand slid the length of my body, rounding my ass as he yanked my lower body to his.

The scent of him swallowed me whole, soap, the remnants of his cologne, and Jai. He made love to my mouth as our slick skin slid against each other. His hands roamed my body, memorizing every curve with his fingertips. Pulling back from my mouth, he kissed his way down my chin and neck until he reached a breast. I slid my hands into his hair and massaged his head in rhythm with his tongue.

Easing himself up, he straddled my hips and stared at me. Those dark brown eyes swallowed me whole, filled with so many emotions I couldn't pick a single one out. Everything his eyes said poured into my heart, a wordless conversation I didn't need to hear, but needed to feel.

Placing a hand on his shoulder, I rolled him over and in turn straddled him. I cupped the side of his face with my hand and dotted his lips with tender kisses. Through simple touches we said much more than any words could say. We shared an understanding, and one night to express it.

He reached into the drawer next to his bed and pulled out a condom, ripping it open with speed and determination. With a smile, I took it and unrolled it over him.

A sly grin ghosted his lips as he grabbed my waist and flipped me over onto the bed. Leaning forward, he raked his hands down my body, stopping to massage my breasts before dragging his hands along my belly to my thighs. One hand disappeared between my legs, and with one long, drawn out stroke he forced a gasping moan from my lungs. Determined fingers worked to bring me to the edge until I cried out his name as his fingers spun my world upside down.

"Jai," I groaned. My hips rocked, matching the speed of his fingertips.

"There it is," he said, leaning over my body until he kissed along my ear. "You have the most magnificent O face I've ever seen. I wish you could see how beautiful you are."

I forced back a series of gasps as my orgasm faded. He dragged his gaze from my eyes, to my lips and back. "I'll never forget this night for the rest of my life. You really have no idea how I feel about you."

I opened my lips to speak, but he placed a finger over them hushing me. My own scent hit my nose, and a flutter hit my belly, arousing me again. Pursing my lips, I kissed his fingertip, before sucking it into my mouth. His eyes drooped to a close, and a soft moan rumbled in his throat as he eased himself inside me.

He pressed a hand to my pelvis as he rocked his hips with a sensual undulation. His movements were like a dance, each one purpose-driven and intent. I lost myself watching him, falling deeper into an almost dream-like state of absolute pleasure. I'd never experienced such intense ecstasy.

I fought to keep my eyes open. I wanted to keep watching him, but the pleasure overwhelmed me. As I closed my eyes, his lips melted with mine as his rhythm increased. Our hands clasped together and he held my arms above my head as a low growl rumbled from his chest. A gasping moan burst from my lips, breaking our kiss.

He nuzzled his face against my neck forcing a giggle out of me. "You made me close my eyes, and I missed your second O face. We'll just have to do it again."

My heart fluttered all the way to my belly. Thoughts of doing that again with him already had my nethers ready to go, and he was still inside me. Then the realization fully hit that Jai was inside me. We just made love.

Tonight had been such a whirlwind, a blur. He went from the bane of my existence, to my rescuer, to the love of my life in a single night. Then the knife of reality sliced through as I remembered it would be only one single night.

I unclasped our hands and wrapped my arms around him so tight the circulation in my arms almost cut off. He slid his arms under me and wrapped me in his own tight embrace. We laid there like that for what felt like forever. Until the thoughts refused to stop circulating in my head and tears splashed my cheeks.

"Hey," he said, pressing his lips to one of the tears. "Was I that bad?"

A laugh burst from my lips and I almost snorted. "Bad? That was like right out of Kama Sutra or something."

Even his smugness turned my arousal on full blast. "Well, I

am Indian. Maybe it's in the blood."

I shoved his shoulder with a laugh. His eyes narrowed and he dove at my neck, sucking in my flesh between his tongue and teeth. A gasp ripped from my lungs, and I writhed under him.

"Careful or I really will go for round two," he said against my ear.

"I dare you." I dragged my hands along his lower back until I got to his ass and squeezed.

"Don't ever dare me." He flipped me over, rolled to his side, pulled me against his chest, and raised my thigh to rest on top of his. Slipping his fingers inside me, I drowned in that euphoric ecstasy. My breathing sped in time with my thundering heart as he brought me just to the edge then stopped.

"No. For the love of God don't stop!" I blinked and rolled my head to look him in the eyes. But he crawled out from behind me.

"Oh, I'm not done with you yet." He pressed my thighs open, and his face disappeared between them. His tongue slid inside me, replacing his fingers. Noises even I didn't know I could make echoed through the room. One of his hands shot to my breast, and massaged it in time with his tongue as he finished me off with his mouth. He fed on me with fervor, like he couldn't get enough. I thought of no better way to die than for him to suck all the pleasure from my body.

Because at the end of it all, my heart would break and I'm not sure I'd be able to come back from it.

CHAPTER 16

JAI

I buried myself in her hoping that somehow I could just drown and take my impending doom of a future with me. Cat was like a drug, and I wanted to overdose. I tried. I tried so hard to fight it. But one night of ecstasy with her would be better than a lifetime of regret and what ifs. Or so I thought. The minute it was over, the longing for more started. And a whole new fight began.

Kissing my way back up her trembling body, I nestled her in my arms and held onto her for fear she'd disappear and take my heart with her.

"Are you happily sated or do I need to tap back into my Kama Sutra bag of tricks?"

She wiggled against me, pressing her back to my chest releasing a long sigh. I trailed a finger along her thigh with one hand, holding firm to her breast with the other tucked around her.

"I'm happily spent." She ran a hand along mine, weaving in and out of my fingers covering her breast.

Her hair tickled my nose, and I placed soft kisses against her head with a smile and drifted off to the deepest sleep I'd had in a very long time. Cat filled my dreams all night. Those dreams where it feels they're so real when you wake up. Near the end of one, we were making love and she went down on me.

I woke up, rocking my hips with a loud groan to find Cat's mouth at the end of my dick. I blinked, wondering if I remained in a dream or if I truly just woke up to Cat giving me a blow job. But the moment her mouth tightened around me and gave one long suck, it was as real as the cum about to shoot right out of me.

"Cat, baby, stop. I'm gonna come," I groaned.

But she refused and kept her mouth planted around my dick. The minute her tongue slid back down my shaft, I was done for, and a shiver ravaged my body so hard I gripped my headboard and nightstand to hold me down.

Heavy breaths labored in my lungs, like I'd just hiked the side of a mountain. Holy fuck. I'd never experienced an orgasm that outright exhausted me. The little minx crawled her way up my body until she straddled me. I forced my eyes back open, and the most gorgeous smile burst from her lips.

"Morning." Leaning in, she swept my mouth into a delicious kiss. I prayed I didn't have morning breath.

I cradled her in my arms and rolled her to my side, staring into her eyes as I shook my head. "Well that was an incredible thing to wake up to. I seriously thought I was still dreaming."

"You were dreaming about me?" Sunlight filtered into the room through the slats in the blinds, hitting her dark honey-colored eyes. They sparkled with happiness. She actually enjoyed herself. I didn't even think girls liked giving BJs. I'd give anything to be able to wake up to her face every morning.

"I have every night since we met." I brushed a lock of hair from her face.

"Give me your camera," she said.

I arched a brow. "Is that how you ask?"

"Oh, I'm sorry." Pressing her lips against my chest, she dragged her tongue over my nipple all the way up my neck to my lips. Tugging my bottom lip between hers, she sucked on it as she stared into my eyes before releasing it.. "May I please borrow your camera?"

"I think," I choked out. "I think I need to punish you some more for your lack of manners."

Dragging her breasts along my chest, she reached over me and grabbed the camera from the nightstand. "There, now you can punish me properly for taking your things."

My heart raced at the thought. What if she wanted me to spank her? Oh, how I wanted to spank her. Shit, was she into kinky sex? I wondered if Mick had any handcuffs.

Fuck, what the hell am I thinking?

"Smile," she said, distracting me from my thoughts as she took a selfie of us with my camera. "You know, if we never get out of bed, then the day doesn't have to start and it's still considered one night." She wrapped a thigh around mine and tugged my waist to hers.

I let out a laugh. She truly didn't want it to end. Nor did I. But prolonging it would only make it harder. If we made love again, it would be damn near impossible. As it was, I seriously contemplated running away with her and leaving Kanti at the altar. Not that her lesbian lover wouldn't be there to dry her fake tears.

To go against my family and refuse this marriage would shame them, and me. The irony of it all, how would I know if she was in love with me unless we tried to have a relationship. But having a relationship would mean broken hearts in the end if I couldn't convince my parents to drop the arranged marriage. If I chose Cat over my family, I'd lose them. No matter what direction I chose, someone would get hurt.

I let out a long sigh. "I know. But you should probably let your family know you're okay. I'm sure by now the word has spread about the storm on all the news outlets. I should probably let mine know as well."

She gave a nod. "Yeah. You're right. I should call them, except everything I own is back in the dorm, and I can't even get in there."

"Here, you can use my phone." I handed her my phone after unlocking the screen.

She stared at the phone, then back at me. "You have me as your wallpaper?"

My heart plunged to my gut. I completely forgot I put the picture of her from yesterday in my batman shirt and glasses on my phone after she sent it to me as Impossible Girl. I about slapped myself and could only respond with the deer-in-the-headlights look.

She bit her lip and tilted her head. Pressing her smiling mouth to mine, she thanked me profusely with her tongue. I guessed she liked it. Without thinking, I wrapped her up in my arms, and the phone dropped to the floor as I got lost in her kisses.

I wanted to stay lost in them forever and deeply considered her offer to just stay in bed when a knock at the door pulled me back to reality.

"Jai? You guys up?" Mick asked through the door.

I pulled back with reluctance and let out a sigh. "Yeah, what's up?"

"Can I come in?" He cleared his throat.

I quirked a brow and tucked myself and Cat under a mound of blankets. "Yeah, sure."

Mick slid around the door. "Dude, your parents are here."

My eyes all but bugged out of my head. "Say what?"

Mick nodded. "Apparently they heard about the tornado and drove up. And guess who's here with them?"

"No."

"Yes."

"Who?" Cat piped up.

Shit.

"Kanti." Mick folded his arms as he leaned on the door.

"Fuck." I fell backwards onto my pillow.

"And they're staying, since your birthday party is Friday night anyway. So, you may want to hurry this along before they come up here and find you. I'm doing my best to stall them, but you know if you're not down there in five minutes your mother will come up here." Mick gave a tilt of his head. "Mornin' Cat." And he slipped out the door.

"Shit. Shit. Shit." I ran a hand down my face and rolled my head to face Cat. "I'm so, so sorry."

"Why didn't you tell me about your birthday?" Her pretty pouty lips almost made me forget about my parents. Of all things, she picked *that* out of the conversation.

"Well, you know, we had that thing with the sociology papers, then the tornado thing, then the making love thing … wasn't really thinking about my birthday."

"Well, we could pretend that I'm one of the other guy's

girlfriends or something," she suggested.

"Right. Wearing my clothes? We were supposed to take you shopping today to get some things."

"Well, do you have anything not so geeky that they wouldn't know was yours? Like just a plain shirt?" She jumped out of the bed and wandered to my closet.

I followed her, watching her ass shake as she scampered to the closet. Dammit if my dick didn't rise to the occasion just looking at her naked in front of me.

"I thought you liked geeky?" I slid my arms around her from behind.

"I do. But if I go downstairs in your hulk t-shirt, they're going to know. How about this one?" She pulled out a plain black t-shirt and slipped it over her stunning breasts.

My heart pouted, sad to see them covered. "Looks better on you than it does on me."

"No one—I mean no one—can fill out a shirt like you can, Jai. You have zero competition."

I tried to hide a smile at her compliment. "Here, my smallest pair of shorts. Hopefully they'll stay up on you long enough to make it to the store. Stay out of the water with them. I don't want you having a wardrobe malfunction the middle of town." I tossed her a wink and helped her into the shorts.

She grabbed my hand and clasped our fingers together. Biting her lip, tears slipped over her cheeks. My heart broke in two. Not only because I hated seeing her cry, but knowing I was the one making her cry.

Slipping a finger under her chin, I looked into her eyes. "I will never forget last night. Or this morning. Ever. This really, really sucks."

"I know. I thought … I dunno. I thought maybe … " She shifted from one foot to the other, tightening her grip on my fingers. "I didn't think it would be this hard to say goodbye." She blew out a hard breath and dropped my hand. I didn't even get to kiss her goodbye.

I think I needed that kiss more than she did. Shit. Water filled my eyes like I just snorted an onion. What the actual fuck? Was I crying?

I wiped the tears from my leaking eyes and huffed out a deep breath. I threw on some clothes and made my way down the stairs to my inevitable demise.

"Jaidev!" My mother threw her arms around me. "We were so worried."

I gave her a terse pat and pulled out of the hug. "I'm fine."

"This girl. This Cat, she's the one you rescued last night?" She pointed to Cat sitting at the kitchen table with Angie picking at a bowl of cereal.

I nodded, unsure what Mick or any of them had told my folks. "Yeah."

"I'm so proud of you. You showed honor and bravery." My father cupped his hand on my shoulder, giving it a tight squeeze.

"Thanks." Intermittent stares between me and Cat became our only form of communication. The pain in her eyes mirrored that in my heart.

Kanti walked in from the bathroom in the hallway. "Hey Jai." She wrapped her arms around me in a hug. "Kanti." I gave my friend a hug and whispered into her ear. "She's the one in the black."

Kanti smiled and winked, mouthing the words *I know*.

Marrying one of my best friends wouldn't be the end of the world. Her being a vagitarian kind of ruined it though, and the fact that I was in love with Cat. But Kanti understood me better sometimes than I did myself. A part of me was glad she was there. Maybe together we could talk some sense into our parents. Not that it would be the first time we tried. But now I had something more to fight for, Cat.

I would have loved to get Kanti and Cat in a room together, hot lesbian threesome fantasies aside. Undoubtedly, they'd end up friends. But how to do that with my parents there?

"Is Maya here with you?"

Kanti lowered her head, speaking out of earshot of my folks. "She's back at the hotel. But, she'll be coming to the party."

"Jai, we need to get you fitted for your birthday suit." My mother walked over and patted down my wrinkled shirt. "I won't have you be seen in wrinkles at your party."

"I'll call the insurance people today. I do hope they plan to replace the window before then." My father studied the blown out window in the front room. "It's not safe."

I rolled my eyes so hard my head throbbed. Half the campus had been destroyed by a tornado and he worried about one window. Far greater concerns now plagued the campus, like Cat's entire building. Where would she be staying in the meantime? With my parents coming and going over the next week until my birthday, staying here was no longer an option.

"You know, with the whole clean up from the storm going on, I think maybe we should hold off on a party for me. Seems in bad form to throw a huge bash when there are so many people displaced and in chaos." Not only Cat, but a good portion of the student body now had to find new housing. The idea of a kegger in the midst of it just didn't seem right.

Not that a party my parents would throw would be a kegger. It would be filled with a shit-ton of Indian cuisine, music only I'd heard of—sans the stuff I forced Mick to listen to—and the ever-present awkwardness of my parents judging my friends. I'd already caught mom giving Cat and Angie the stink-eye in the kitchen, and I could only imagine what kind of thoughts ran through her mind. Mainly because Cat didn't have a bra on. Believe me, no one could miss her fantastic perky breasts.

"Why don't we turn it into a fundraiser?" Cat piped up walking in from the kitchen.

I spun around and locked eyes with her. Her warm smile filled the room the minute she walked in. Or maybe it was the heat welling inside me thinking that moments ago she lay in my bed naked and I had the most fantastic sex of my life.

Dude, what is wrong with me? My parents are right here!

"That's not a bad idea." I beckoned Cat to come forward. "Mother, Father, this is Catherine Marek. She goes by Cat."

"We met briefly earlier. Pleasure to meet you." She extended her hand to my mother and father, but dad refused to shake, addressing her only with a slight nod. "Thanks to your son, I'm still alive. He was very brave. I'll be forever indebted to him."

Mother gave a terse nod. "Catherine, have you met Kanti? She and Jaidev are to be married."

Just put a stake in me.

It took everything in my power not to grab Cat and run out the door. The more my parents acted outrageous, the more the idea appealed to me.

Cat faced the situation with a graceful smile, not missing a beat. "Ah, yes, Kanti." She extended her hand. "Jai's told me about you. You're even more beautiful in person than in the picture."

Mom beamed, probably thinking I'd come around to the idea of the arranged marriage since I'd talked about it to Cat.

"Oh? Jai showed you a picture of me?" Kanti shot me a smirk. "It's nice to know my future husband has a picture of me."

My middle finger kept inching its way up. She could be such a brat.

"Well, perhaps this fundraiser idea would be beneficial. I'll talk with Sanjeet and see about making a donation from our office to get it started." My father pulled out his phone and sent a message to Kanti's father.

"I'll have to notify the caterer. We'll need more food." Mom busted out her phone and started making arrangements. If nothing else, we Indians knew how to throw a party.

In the distraction, I pulled Cat into the kitchen, out of their line of sight. I slid a hand along her neck and pulled her face to mine, sweeping her lips into a kiss. Pressing against her mouth with fervor, I tried to tell her everything I wanted to say upstairs but never got the chance. Hopefully she understood.

A soft moan floated through the kiss as she curled her fingers into my hair. I loved it when she did that. Tingles radiated down to my toes. She completely undid me.

Kanti jerked to a stop at the kitchen door. From the corner of my eye, I caught a blazing smile on her lips as she watched us.

"Jaidev, where did you go?" My father bellowed from the front room.

"He's just grabbing a bite," Kanti said with a smile and stood guardian at the door.

That was why she was my best friend.

With reluctance, I pulled back from the kiss and reached into my pocket. "Here, take my phone. I don't want you without a way to call your parents. And, I want to be able to get hold of you and know you're okay." I shoved the phone into the pocket of her shorts, well my shorts. "If you get a call from Mick's phone it's me."

"Jai … " She shook her head.

I pressed a finger to her gorgeous kiss-swollen lips. "Don't argue. Take my credit card and get a few things. Don't go wild or anything, but get at least a couple of changes of clothes. Go to the store with Angie. We'll find somewhere to put you up until housing contacts you. I'll double with Mick and you two can have my room."

So much for ending things. This would be a lot harder than I ever imagined.

CHAPTER 17

CAT

Angie grabbed my arm and dragged me from the kitchen, my fingertips still touching my kiss-swollen lips. What did that kiss mean? Was it goodbye, or we're going to find a way to make this work?

God bless Kanti. In my heart of hearts I apologized profusely for calling her Indian Barbie. Though with her gorgeous dark-brown perfect hair, flawless olive skin and exotic eyes, she pretty much bitch-slapped Barbie with one look, and any other woman who walked into the room. A long fuchsia dress covered her slender frame. The bottom flared out, adorned with orange trim and beads. Some kind of matching shawl or sash draped one shoulder. I'd never seen a woman more stunning, right down to her perfectly manicured feet in peep-toe wedges.

How in the world Jai wouldn't want to tap that was beyond me. She even made *my* nethers tingle a bit, and I was solidly team peen. But she must be just as opposed to this marriage as Jai, because what other woman would stand guard while her *fiancé* made out with another girl? The fact that he stood in the kitchen kissing me, and not her, blew my mind. It just didn't make sense that if neither party wanted to get married that their parents would force them. The concept was so foreign to me I still couldn't wrap my brain around it.

"Maybe Kanti would like to join you ladies for a girl's day of shopping?" Jai nodded to Kanti on our way out.

"That would be lovely, if you'll have me." Kanti gave me a wink and a smile.

Angie and I look at each other and shrugged.

"Sure, if you'd like," I said.

"You don't need Kanti for anything, Mother, do you?" Jai asked.

His mother pursed her lips and looked between me and Angie. Disdain radiated from her eyes behind her glasses. If they'd been lasers I'd be a hole in the floor. Harsh much?

"It's Kanti's choice. Though, I don't believe her mother would approve of her gallivanting around town—"

"—Perfect! Let's go ladies!" Kanti said, already halfway out the door.

Maybe she wanted away from mommy-dearest as much as I did. Even if Jai and I somehow found a way to make a relationship work, I'd have to deal with the mother-in-law from hell, apparently. Maybe it was for the best.

We climbed into the car, and I stared out the window at Jai standing in the doorway with a smile plastered to his face. What the hell was he up to?

The minute we were down the street Kanti stripped in the backseat.

"What in the world?" I blinked, not even pretending not to stare.

"Sorry, I need out of this salwar kameez." Under her garments she revealed a Pink tour t-shirt and jeans. "Jai's family, well, and mine, are old-fashioned. So around them I try to stay in character. Forgive me."

Still blinking, I nodded. She scooted forward and placed a hand on my shoulder. "Can we swing by our hotel and pick up my girlfriend Maya?"

I nodded at Angie. "Would that be cool with you?"

Angie laughed. "Sure, haven't had a real girl's day in a while. I'm game."

"Thank you so much." Kanti slipped her arms around

my shoulders from behind and gave me a tight squeeze before slipping back into her seat. "I feel like I know you already. Jai hasn't stopped talking about you."

Kanti's bubbly spirit grew on me. As much as I wanted to loathe her for marrying my almost-would-be boyfriend, I kind of liked her. Especially when she told me that he told her all about me.

"So, what do you do, Kanti?" Angie asked, tossing her a glance in the rearview mirror.

"Right now, I help my mother run an in-home daycare. I really want to be a singer though." She stared out the passenger window with a sigh.

"Have you done anything to pursue that as a career?" I asked.

"No. I really wanted to go Bollywood. But the women from my mom's culture would never approve. They don't tend to work outside the home much. I thought that once we moved to the U.S. things would be different. They would see how life is here. Modern. But because they grew up in a small village in India, they still hold to old cultural beliefs." The more upset she got the more her mixed British and Indian accent came out as I studied her lips in the rear-view mirror.

"Have you or Jai ever expressed your feelings against the marriage?" Angie asked. God love her, I was too focused on thinking about Jai to even bring it up.

"Several times over the years. But it is always the same answer. It will be good for the families. Our fathers are business partners. They trust each other's family. And know we will be a good match." She let out a half-laugh, half-snort.

I turned in my seat to look her in the eyes. "There's no way to just say no, and not go through with it? How can they physically force you to get married?"

"They can't. But if we do not, then we will dishonor the family. Indian families have done this for hundreds of years. It is their right to choose the match for their children to ensure wealth, health and honor. Going against that is going against your parents and their judgment. Shaming them. The idea of romantic marriage is just in Bollywood movies. A Western ideal."

"Then why did you all move here, to the Western world?"

Angie asked.

"Economic reasons. Job opportunities for our fathers. But living here does not mean we adapt to the Western way of living, or even thinking. Even Jai will have to give up his photojournalism dream and take on a role in our fathers' medical practice."

My gut wrenched at the thought of what I was up against. I would truly lose Jai forever. And Jai would lose himself. He loved photography. His life's dream. He spoke so passionately of it, almost as passionately as his kisses. I'd seen him in action. He had a gift. A gift that would be wasted when the world needed to see it. How could a parent rip away their child's dream?

Angie pulled into the hotel parking lot.

"Just drive around out front, I told Maya to be waiting outside. No time to lose," Kanti said, unbuckling her seatbelt.

No time to lose for what? Before Angie ever got the car in park, Kanti leapt out the door and ran over to a pretty blonde girl in a red long-sleeve sweater and jeans. They crashed together, and Kanti laid a kiss on the girl so powerful it made my heart leap into my throat just watching it.

Holy. Shit. Kanti was a lesbian. My eyes doubled in size.

So did Angie's as she turned to me. "Did you just see what I just saw?"

Words lodged in the back of my throat, only managing to respond with a nod.

"Well that explains why she wasn't overly bothered by Jai laying one on you in the kitchen." Angie snorted.

The situation just leveled up. Kanti, a closet lesbian was being forced to marry Jai, my kind-of-sort-of-but-not-really boyfriend. Well no wonder why Jai said he had no interest in her romantically. I nodded to myself as I put all the puzzle pieces in place. He wanted Kanti to go shopping with us so she could spend time with her girlfriend. Holy hell, she actually even said girlfriend. I just thought she meant girl friend.

We had to fix this. We had to. Everything about this fake marriage was so wrong. Bile lurched into my throat.

Kanti helped Maya into the car, snuggling as close to her as humanly possibly. "Girls, this is Maya."

I tossed Maya a wave and a smile. "Pleasure to meet you."

"Thank you so much for letting us have the day together. I didn't think I'd get to see Kanti at all until the party. I had to drive up here and hide out, sneaking kisses in the hall at midnight just to see her." Maya slid a hand along Kanti's cheek. Such adoration and love poured out of her words and reflected in her eyes as she looked at her lover. I sympathized with them.

"I had no fucking idea you were a lesbian," Angie blurted out. Sometimes she was so less than tactful.

"Jai never told you?" Kanti tilted her head and placed a hand on my shoulder.

I shook my head. "No."

"That boy. Do not take it out on him. I swore him to absolute secrecy about it since we were ten years old. If anyone found out ... well ... " Kanti's eyes glassed over.

Maya wiped a tear slipping over Kanti's cheek. "What she's trying to say is, homosexuality is still punishable by law in India. And even though she lives here now, we don't know how her parents would react to the thought of it. It's still taboo in their culture."

"How long have you two been together?" I asked.

"Three years." Kanti gave Maya's hand a tight squeeze.

Jai and I had barely been together a speck in time in comparison, and if they felt for each other half as much as I did for Jai ... I couldn't even imagine going through that for three years.

We got to the mall, and it was less crowded than I imagined it would be. Probably because half the town still spent the majority of their time cleaning up from the storm.

"You guys go in, I'm going to sit out here and just give my folks a call real quick." Popping a squat on a nearby planter, I swiped at the screen-saver, and my face smiled back at me.

I still couldn't believe he put my picture on his phone.

"He's fallen for you hard, you know that right?" Kanti took a seat next to me.

"It just doesn't seem real. He doesn't seem real. Like something out of my imagination of the perfect guy." I shook my head.

"Yeah. He's one of the good ones. Believe me, I'd be clawing your eyes out right now if we were a real couple." Kanti let out a laugh. "But he's like my brother, and my best friend. He tells me pretty much everything. And, I have never seen him like this over any other girl, ever."

Kanti certainly didn't help the situation telling me inside intel. Any other time this would have been awesome to know what he'd said or was thinking. But it only made it harder.

"I can see why he likes you. You're gorgeous. That idea about the fundraiser was generous and kind. And apparently you understand this American football thing, drink disgusting beer, and know what he's talking about when he names every comic book figure known to man. That takes a special kind of person."

I let out a snort. "Well, we all have to have a hobby."

"I want you to know, I hope you guys still remain friends. After our wedding I mean. I will not force you to stay away, even if his mother wants you to. Jai and I, we sort of have this pact. I'm not giving up Maya, so I won't make him give you up." She rubbed her hands in a nervous jitter along her jeans.

"Won't that just be weird? I mean, that's living a lie. I can't fathom having to lead a secret life under the pretense that it's to preserve culture. What kind of values? How is any of this right?"

Sure I ached to be with Jai, but to have to sneak around like having an affair, I didn't know if I could bear it.

"Well, it would be harder if we actually lived back in India. But here it'll be a little easier. While we still hold to our cultural beliefs, we can also incorporate some Western ideals. Some things are easier to pass off, or not pay attention to. I mean, if I go back to India, and someone finds out I'm gay, I could actually be put in jail. So, I'm just thankful we're staying over here."

"That's insane. Why can't people just love who they want to love? Love is the most powerful and beautiful thing in the world."

Kanti gave my hand a pat. "Because human nature is to fear something you don't understand. It's the million dollar question."

I nodded, releasing a small sigh. Frustration boiled in my veins. I felt powerless to do anything.

"I know it's not ideal. But we can try and make the best of the situation. I hope you think about my offer to still remain in Jai's life." She left me to my thoughts as she ducked inside the store.

Would I give up my own values just to keep Jai in my life? Could I continue to be in a relationship with him if he was married to someone else? Even with it being a non-romantic marriage, he would be legally someone else's. The thought of laying in his arms, giving myself to him physically and emotionally, then never being able to have him give me all of himself in return just didn't sit well with me.

Ugh. I ran my hands through my hair and tried to make sense of all the thoughts jumbled in my head. But their marriage was just a piece of paper. Why let a piece of paper tell me who I could or couldn't love? I suddenly understood the plight of the LGBT community fighting for marriage equality. The battles they faced every day in my own country, and around the world.

All I wanted to do was love Jai, but everything in the universe seemed to want to stop me.

CHAPTER 18

JAI

I buried my face in the pillow she'd slept on, drinking in her scent that still lingered. Maybe I should have told her how I felt. But saying the words out loud would only make it hurt more, knowing nothing would ever come of us.

I hoped I was good last night. She seemed to enjoy it. Hell, I did. Maybe when you're in love the sex is just that much better. Not that I was all that experienced in sex. Sure, I'd gotten my fair share of lays in college. Mostly drunk chicks after a frat party just looking to get off. But it at least helped with the sexual frustration of not having a steady girlfriend.

I never allowed myself to have one at all during the last four years since the impending marriage had been arranged. While yeah, I still wanted to get laid, I didn't want to hurt anyone knowing it couldn't really go anywhere past a bed buddy. But Cat, man, she spun me for a loop. From the moment I laid eyes on her, I knew she was different. I kept trying to deny it, but fuck if she didn't just tear up every plan I ever made.

Then to find out she was actually Impossible Girl? The girl I planned on keeping for myself after my marriage to Kanti went through. Kanti and I had agreed that she would have her secret lover, Maya, and I would find someone for me. But who would want to be in a messed up relationship like that? I didn't know that I could even fathom attempting it myself. But at least with IG, keeping it online made it simpler.

Everything was so fucked up. I was in love for the first time in my life, and there wasn't a damned thing I could do about it. We should never have made love. A chest-caving ache sliced open my heart and broke in two every time I thought about it. They say better to have loved and lost than to never have loved at all.

Fuck that. I call bullshit. It sucked ass.

I had to stop myself from logging onto the computer and messaging IG. Because this would be the very thing I'd go to her to forget. Only now, IG was the thing I was trying to forget. Stuffing a pillow over my face, I rolled over and tried to close my eyes to sleep these ridiculous chick emotions off. I felt like a wussy baby. Men didn't wallow. Men didn't cry over a chick. My dad would beat my ever loving ass if he knew I sat up here pining for Cat.

Even if the marriage bomb didn't factor in, just the look in Mom's eyes as she sized up Cat was enough to say Kanti or not, Cat would never be accepted into my life.

I rolled to the edge of the bed and sat up, dropping my head in my hands. Cat and the girls would be back soon, and I'd have to spend the next several days with her here in the house, trying to manage to stay clear.

I picked up my camera and stared at the picture Cat took of us in bed this morning. Her head nuzzled into my shoulder, and my arms wrapped around her tight as she took a selfie of us. An unmistakable smile plastered over my lips. I hadn't smiled in a picture in years. Right there before my eyes, the epitome of happiness. I had it for a brief moment in time.

Ignoring Cat would be hard. Forgetting her entirely would be damn near impossible. My Impossible Girl. I hit delete on the picture and erased my happiness. Time to channel the ultimate friend zone.

I tossed the camera on the bed and ran back down the stairs. Everything about this house suffocated me with memories of her. I needed air.

"Ah, Jaidev, I was looking for you. Chandar is here to work on your suit for the birthday party." My mother tugged at my elbow and shoved me toward a little man with a tape measure wrapped around his neck like a coiled up cobra.

"Mom, I don't want to wear a suit. I want a casual party. It's a fundraiser now, not even *my* party anymore." The last thing I wanted to do on my birthday was get stuck in a stuffy suit. All I did was please everyone else. Could I not have one thing that made me happy in my life?

Mother sat on the sofa, flipping through her party planner. "I will not have my son go out looking like rubbish. Stand still."

Frustration and anger boiled in my mind. I closed my eyes and sucked in a deep breath, but Cat flashed before me every single time.

"I think we should move the wedding up to December. Just have it when we go to India on your break. Your father will be traveling back and forth to New Orleans most of the summer, so trying to have it then will only make things more stressful." Mother never even looked up from her planner, like the Mac truck she just drove over me with didn't shatter my whole world.

"No. In fact, NO! I don't want to get married at all. I'm in love with Cat." The words flew out of my mouth before I could stop them.

Mother finally looked at me. "I know you are. Another very good reason to move the wedding up sooner."

I shook my head. "What? What do you mean you know I am?"

"I am your mother, Jaidev. I know you better than you know yourself. The look in your eyes when you look at her says more than words." The curt snap of her flipping pages ticked in my ears like a bomb.

"You know I'm in love with her and you're still forcing me to marry Kanti?" I dropped to my knees in front of her and pleaded with my eyes.

"She is not right for you. Kanti will make a good wife, a good mother to your children. This Cat person reeks of lust and disrespect. She can't even walk around in proper attire."

"Mom, she was in a tornado last night. I rescued her in her pajamas! She didn't have time to stop and put on a bra as glass shattered around us, walls crumbled like pie crust, and the floor just about caved beneath our feet."

Rage. I'd never experienced it before, and it churned inside me like a bubbling volcano. One more thing and I'd explode.

Mother pursed her lips, narrowing her eyes. "It matters not. I'm very proud of you for saving another's life. But the wedding will go on as planned. Does this Cat even love you back?"

I swallowed over the lump lodged in my throat. "Yeah. I'm pretty sure she does."

She shook her head. "Pretty sure? How can you love her and not even know how she feels about you? This is why we make the arrangements for you. Love clouds judgment. You cannot make clear necessary decisions when there is an emotional attachment. We see the bigger picture. We know what's best for you."

"Love doesn't cloud judgment. Okay, sometimes yes. But that's the beauty of it." I threw my hands up. "It makes us do extraordinary things. I ran clear across campus in a tornado to rescue the girl I love. I saved her life because of it." I rocked back and sat on the floor. "She makes me happy."

"Only temporarily. Love falters. Emotions grow weary over time, and those euphoric feelings you have now will fade." She placed a hand on my shoulder. "I, too, was once in love. It broke my heart to let Ruslaan go when I had to marry your father. But I know it was the right decision. You will get over it in time. Time is stronger than all things else."

Ugh, now she spouted old Indian proverbs. Because that would suddenly make me change my mind. Short of telling them Kanti was gay, nothing would prevent the wedding from taking place. And even then, I'm not so sure they wouldn't still make me marry her so that they could hide her homosexuality from the world under the guise of this marriage. When we'd have to turkey baste my swimmers into her to get a baby, would they finally understand my plight?

Mick came in, arms loaded with cases of beer. I needed a drink. Or the entire case.

"Want a cold one?" Mick asked.

I nodded and grabbed one from him, chugging it back in four gulps.

"Jaidev!" Mother scolded.

"Are we done here?" I asked the tailor dude.

He nodded and waved me off. I grabbed the case of beer Mick just put in the fridge and slammed the back door behind me. I made my way to the fire pit in the far corner of the backyard and plopped into one of the lawn chairs. As I cracked open another beer, Mick curled his hand over my shoulder.

"Can I get at least one of the beers I just bought?" He smiled, grabbed one out of the case and sat in one of the chairs across from me.

"Sorry, man. I'll buy you a new case tonight. I promise." I slammed back another beer and tossed it to the ground.

"Parents still not letting up on the marriage thing, huh?" Mick took a small swig of his beer, while I pile-drived a third down my throat. In the midst of everything, blacking out drunk seemed like an awesome plan.

"Yes. Just kill me now." I popped open a fourth beer and tried to drink it, but I couldn't stomach it. The thought of it all becoming real now made me wretch.

"I don't think getting drunk's gonna solve it." Mick grabbed the case of beer from my arms.

I huffed and leaned forward on my elbows. "No, but maybe it'll numb it. They want to move the wedding to December instead of July."

"Dude, that's in a month." Mick's eyes bugged out of his head.

"Yes, I realize this." I dug in my pocket for my phone to check the time and forgot I'd given it to Cat. "Ugh. Maybe I'll just go to my room and watch some porn."

Mick shook his head. "You wanna go for a drive or something? Get away for a while?"

"Naw. Actually, I'm going to go see if I can be of any help with the clean up on campus. Also see if we can get into Cat's building and get her things." I stood up and downed the last of the beer before tossing the cans in the trash.

"I'll come with you. I'm sure they could use a hand. And if we can get in I'll let Angie know, too." Mick dropped the beer in the fridge in the storage shed. At a college house you could never have too many refrigerators.

"I'm gonna run up to my room. I want to take some photos of the aftermath. I'll meet you out front." I jogged up the stairs to grab my camera.

As I opened the door, my father spun around with my camera in his hand. The glare in his eyes ripped a hole in my soul. I assumed he found the pics I took of Cat.

"Your mother tells me you're in love with this girl?" He pointed to the picture of Cat wearing my white shirt. The sunlight filtering through the blinds diffused in the white shirt, shrouding her in a halo of light. My angel.

"Yes. Can I have my camera back? I need to go help with the cleanup and take some pics before it gets dark." I held out my hand waiting for him to turn it over.

"I allowed you to take photography as a hobby, not as your major. You refused medical school, so you were to at least take some business courses. And this is how I find you spending your time? This is trash, Jaidev."

"That's *love*, dad."

He shook his head. "You know nothing of love."

"Neither do you." I grabbed my camera and bolted out of the room. The beer in my stomach bubbled, trying to make a resurgence. Never in my life had I ever spoken to my father like that.

What the hell was wrong with me?

I tore out the door and blazed right passed Mick, who struggled to keep up with me as I ran across campus like the zombie apocalypse chased after me.

"Dude, slow down." Mick wheezed as she shouted behind me.

I jerked to a stop as the north side of campus came into view, and the chaos that surrounded it. The wind still howled in my ears, roaring like a train barreling down on me and Cat. My back tingled as the memory of the glass shattering and slicing through my shirt haunted me as if it just happened. You never forget something like that. No wonder why Cat was so scared. Her first tornado she lost her hearing. If I hadn't been there, she may have lost her life in this one.

Holding the camera to my face to hide the welling tears, I

snapped pictures of everything around me. I didn't care what it was, who it was, or what was left of it. That familiar sound of the camera click tethered me back to reality.

Mick still wheezed behind me, trying to catch his breath. "Dude, what the ever loving fuck was that? And why are you not on the track team?" He bent over, slapped his hands to his knees and coughed.

"Had to get out before either I told my family off, or they forced me to get in the car and drive me back to Houston." With each click, my heart hammered until it thumped so loud I thought it may be a heart attack. The scene before me could not be put into words.

Personal belongings littered the grounds, from toiletries to underwear. Shards of what used to be buildings lay in a pile of rubble, and I just prayed no one was trapped under there. Students, teachers, family, and friends dug through the remnants looking for their things.

"Professor Wilkinson," I shouted across the lawn to my Sociology teacher leading one of the cleanup crews. "Is there anything I can do to help?"

"Jaidev." He held out a hand and gripped mine in a firm handshake. "I heard about your heroics last night saving Catherine Marek's life. Very brave and selfless. I wish others had been as lucky. From what I hear, the death toll is now at five."

His words punched me in the gut. Such heartache and terror these people suffered, and I thought this marriage was the most horrible thing that could happen in life. Nothing like a force of nature to put your life in perspective. Even if I had to marry Kanti, Cat was still alive. She'd get to live a life. And I would get to live mine. Whatever that entailed.

CHAPTER 19

CAT

After a day of shopping, we all piled into the car. The drive to the hotel had us all on the edge of our seats. No one wanted to go back to their secret lives. Kanti, Maya, nor me. Sadness hung thick in the air.

Kanti walked Maya to the hotel entrance. Running a hand through Kanti's hair, Maya pulled her into a bittersweet kiss. Tears slicked both their cheeks as they mouthed *I love you*. The one time lip reading felt like an invasion of privacy. But the passion in their body language said it all louder than their words.

Kanti crawled back into the car and redressed herself into her formal wear, swiping at her eyes with furious fingertips.

I handed her a tissue from the box Angie always stored under her seat. "There's no other word to describe how much this all sucks. You and Maya just belong together. I've never seen two people more in love."

Kanti smiled into the rear view mirror. "One day I hope that all people will be free to love who their heart desires. If it does not hurt another person or threaten their life, why must others look down upon the greatest power we have as humans? Love is the driver of all things. Yet it is the most feared."

Angie let out a sigh in tandem with me.

"You've got my vote," Angie said.

I turned back to face Kanti. "Why don't you stay here at the hotel. Get in a little more time with Maya. We'll tell Jai's mom you weren't feeling well and asked that we drop you off to rest."

"Really?" Kanti's lashes fluttered as she processed the thought.

"Why not?" I shrugged.

"Um, okay. Thank you." Kanti lunged at me over the seat and wrapped her arms tight along my shoulders. She even smelled gorgeous. I loved her and hated her at the same time. "Can you text me and let me know when Jai's parents leave to come back to the hotel? I need to make sure I'm back in my room when they arrive."

I nodded. "Oh crap. I don't have my phone. Jai gave me his though. You've got his number, right? Just send him a text."

"Perfect." Kanti gave us each one last hug and scooted out of the car. "I owe you both."

She even ran like a gazelle. Kanti had everything, beauty, brains and a great personality. Yet she'd never have the thing she truly wanted. Freedom to love.

Angie pulled out of the hotel driveway and hit the highway. "Mick just texted me. Said they're letting people into the dorms to get things before dark. We should probably get back."

"Yeah. Let's drop this stuff off at the house and then walk over." With any luck, we'd get in and out without having to interact with Jai's parents. Neither of them liked me, so I didn't expect a lengthy *get to know you* session over tea.

We pulled into the driveway and their black Mercedes sedan still sat out front. Just the idea of having to walk past them sent my stomach spinning. Grabbing our shopping bags, I all but ran to the house and up the stairs managing to avoid both of them. I said a silent thank you for small blessings. And there I did myself in.

A knock at the door startled me. Sucking in a deep breath, I meandered over to it in a slow stroll hoping maybe whoever it was on the other side would go away by the time I got there.

But what if it was Jai?

I sped up to a dash and whipped it open. Jai's mother stood on the other side. She towered over me by a good couple of inches.

Because I needed even more intimidation from her.

Tiny lines creased the outer edges of her hazel eyes. Probably from years of disapproving glares at every decision Jai made. Streaks of silver threaded through locks of dark hair pulled into a neat bun at the back of her head.

"May I speak with you privately?" She clasped her hands together and let them fall against her stomach. I understood where Jai got his handsome looks. His mother was beautiful, and dressed to the nines. Gold threading weaved through the beautiful blue and purple sari that complimented her skin tone.

"Yes." I opened the door wider allowing her entrance to the room.

Flipping her drooping sash over her shoulder, she took a seat on Jai's bed and patted the empty spot next to her. "Please, sit."

Nodding, I walked over and sat next to her.

"Ms. Marek, I know my son thinks he is in love with you. And, I'm sure in his mind he believes it to be real. But Jaidev is still young and does not think with his head. He does not know what is best for him. He doesn't understand that you cannot make decisions based on emotion. This is why his father and I have chosen a wife for him who will be a good match."

The more she talked, the more I had to force myself to remain in the same room with her. Every word she said made me want to run away with Jai and never look back.

"I don't see how forcing two people who don't want to be married to each other is a good match. Perhaps love clouds my judgment, but it also makes me kind and empathetic to the plight of others." Acid laced my words, more than I had intended. But at this point, I had no choice but to lay it on the table.

"You very well may be kind. You do seem to make Jaidev happy. And, for that I thank you. But you are not what is best for him. Love is for the short term. Respect and honor will keep a marriage together."

I hitched a shoulder. "Wait, what? How can you say a marriage out of love won't have respect and honor?"

"Because with love there are emotions. Emotions are irrational and make people think and act differently, without logic.

Just like Jaidev. He would never have talked to me or his father like he has if he hadn't met you." She gave a pat to my hand and even smiled. "Do not worry, I do not blame you for this. This is how love works. I understand this."

If my eyes widened any further they'd suck the Earth into the black hole void that was my mind right now trying to comprehend such inane beliefs. Words bottle-necked in my throat, and I sat there shaking my head.

"He lacks respect toward us because love is ruling him. He is not thinking clearly," she said.

Jai may not be thinking clearly, but I sure as hell was. Our relationship wouldn't go down without a fight. "Love gives him a reason to fight for his dreams. What about what he wants? What about his career, not only this forced marriage? Love is encouragement and support. And from those come respect and honor."

She grinned. "Regardless of what you think, I do like you Catherine. You have spirit. You fight for what you believe in. But so do I. And, I believe Kanti and Jaidev is the right choice. You are still young. You will find someone else to make you happy. Years down the road, you will thank me."

Unable to hold back, words exploded from my mouth. "How can you even say that? Do you have any idea what we're going through? We make each other happy. We bring out the best in each other. Jai's shown me sides of myself long buried. He accepts me for who I am. I accept him for who he is now, and who he wants to become. You can't even do that. Instead you try to force on him what you want. He is not you, nor is he his father. He is Jaidev. He is his own person with a right to make his own decisions." I slammed a balled fist into my hand.

"I understand more than you know." Looking down, she dusted off a spot on her sari. "I, too, was in love once. About your age. His name was Ruslaan. Such a handsome boy. He gave me his heart, and I gave him mine. It was difficult to let him go. I fought almost as hard as you did to get my parents to let us marry each other. But they'd already arranged a marriage with Jaidev's father. It took me many years to see why, but I understand now. Ruslaan and I would not have been a good match. Jaidev's father protects and provides. He is a hard worker. He is an honorable man and takes care of his family."

A part of me sympathized for her. We shared some common ground. I needed to tap into that in order to change her mind. "How do you know Ruslaan wouldn't have done the same? Just because your family didn't pick him, doesn't mean that he wouldn't have loved you 'til your last breath. How could you see into the future and know that he wouldn't have provided a good life for you and your children? How can you judge someone before giving them a chance?"

She glanced to the floor before turning to face me. "Because I trusted my parents to make the right decision for me. If I had chosen love over my family, I would have lost them. Dishonor is far harder to repair than a broken heart."

So it became an all or nothing situation. Choose love, lose your family. "Don't you ever wonder what would have happened if you did? Don't you still think of Ruslaan?"

She nodded. "From time to time. But I am no longer in love with him. Love wanes. It fades. What blazes hot as a fire now, eventually burns itself out. You cannot make good decisions based on an unsteady emotion. You must have a firm foundation to start. Sometimes you even grow to love the person you are paired with. But it's a different kind of love. One not of passion and romance. But of trust and value."

I learned you can't argue without having a common frame of reference. Her words meant nothing to me because I didn't understand them. And my words bounced off her, because she couldn't see past her beliefs. Then it hit me. I couldn't see past my own.

She grabbed my hand and clutched it tight in her own. "Can you honestly say that thirty years from now, even five years from now, you will still feel for Jaidev as you do right in this moment? Burning desire is what drives you right now. You do not know him enough to make a logical decision not based on feelings."

I loved Jai. But some of what she said filtered in and made a little sense. How could I be sure we'd still love each other the same down the road? But no one could see into the future. No one knew if a relationship would last the test of time. That was part of the excitement. An unwritten future. Just because someone plans it all out for you doesn't mean it will go that way or stick to a specific outline.

"I beg of you, Catherine. If you truly love my son and want what's best for him … let him go." Her glassy eyes stared into my own. "I am glad he's had someone in his life to know what love feels like. I am glad you fight for him and want him to be happy. Fight for him in a different way. Fight to make him see he needs to choose a respectful and honorable future. If you want him to be happy, it cannot be with you. Do you want to be his regret that he chose you over his family?"

Her words slapped me in the face and sucked the air from my lungs. The word *regret* gutted me. I didn't want to be anyone's regret, let alone Jai's. I couldn't possibly make him choose me over his family. The entire conversation jumbled in my head. I fought so hard to change her mind, but change it for what purpose? So that I could continue to date her son? So that I could *maybe* one day marry him? So that *maybe* one day end up divorced because we only burned hot because we couldn't be together?

Tears welled in my eyes and spilled over my cheeks. Every last word she said sliced through every single reason I gave her. Doubt became my enemy, and her shield.

She rose from the bed. "Do what you know is the right decision, Catherine. For everyone."

She closed the door behind her and on my last chance with Jai.

CHAPTER 20

JAI

Sweat beaded my brow as I tossed the final load of trash into the dumpster. While the tornado created chaos and destruction, it brought together a community of people and formed a bond. Everyone pitched in and helped with the cleanup. Jocks, geeks, even club Wicca all put their differences aside and became one unit of humanity. I clicked off one last picture.

"Do you know if they're letting anyone back into San Jac Hall?" I asked one of the other professors dumping off a load of wood chunks of what used to be a tree.

"I think so, but only until dusk. And only those with rooms on the south side of the building. They have it blocked off for all the other rooms." Someone yelled out the professor's name behind him. "If you'll excuse me, Jaidev."

I nodded and turned to Mick. "Did you call Angie and let her know we can get in?"

"Yup. Already on it."

"Okay, I'm gonna go ahead and see if I can grab a few of Cat's things. It'll be dark soon, and they may not make it back before they stop letting people in."

"Sounds good. Be careful." Mick nodded and grabbed another handful of debris.

I made my way to the entrance of the hall. A couple people stood watch at the front of a table with a binder.

"Hey Jai," a blonde said from behind the table.

"Um, hey." I shot her a wave, having no idea who she was or how she knew my name.

"You don't remember me, do you?" Her tongue darted over her lips. It kinda skeeved me out.

I hoped my smile looked more sincere than it felt. "Sorry, drawing a blank."

"We met a while back, when you were looking for Cat's room."

Oh right. The boob chick in the hallway the night I found out I was Cat's sociology paper victim. Yeah, she totally looked different in the dark.

"Oh right. Yeah, nice to see you again. Um hey, Cat's in town getting some clothes and things. I need to run up to her room and grab her laptop and phone and see what's left of her stuff. Can I go in?" Time to give her the smolder and hope she'd let me in.

"We're really only supposed to let the actual students who live in the hall in." Giving her hips a swivel, she wandered out from the table and placed a hand on my arm. I developed a sudden need to take a shower to wash away the skeeve. "But, I know you're cool, so I'll let you in if you hurry. Have to be out before dusk. Here take a flashlight, the stairwell is pretty dark."

"I really appreciate it." I took off before she tried to touch me again.

I walked through what was left of the glass doors that used to be the entrance. Twisted chunks of metal arched above me as I passed through. Only the sun lit the hallways, casting shadows into the gray and lifeless building once full of chattering women and bouncing boobs. It was like walking into a graveyard, eerie and bleak.

Sobs of distraught girls echoed through the halls as they picked up the remnants of their lives. I ran up the stairwell, thankful for the flashlight from blondie since Cat had my phone. As I came out on the third floor, that sound played back in my ears of the roaring winds and debris smashing into the building, like a time-warp echo from Doctor Who or something. It freaked me out more than I cared to admit as I relived the anxiety of last night trying to find Cat in the pitch dark. At least this time I had a flashlight. Though the hallway in the day with the light filtering in through the holes in the walls and broken windows helped.

I found her room, door still open from when we left last night. Floorboards creaked beneath my feet as I peered in. The site sucker-punched me in the gut, and I was glad Cat wasn't there to see it. Sunlight hit the shattered glass, reflecting like a thousand tiny diamonds around the room. Branches, clothes, drywall, and bricks lay scattered among the sparkling jewels.

Sucking in a deep breath, I stepped inside. Glass crunched under my shoes as I made my way to her desk to collect her laptop and phone still sitting there, thankfully. I opened her closet and found a duffle bag and stuffed a bunch of clothes and shoes in, not knowing if they were hers or Angie's. Didn't really matter.

I ran to the bathroom to collect some toiletries and jerked to a stop as I hit the darkness. My first kiss with Cat happened in that very room, in the dark. It played over in my mind as I remembered her soft trembling lips pressing against mine as she shook in my arms. But somehow, the moment our mouths met, her body calmed and we both went to another place, another time. She took me to other worlds, my Impossible Girl.

More glass crunched in my ear, but it wasn't from my feet. I spun around as Cat walked into the room.

"Hey." Her voice echoed like a soft whisper.

"Hey," I said back like a dorky caveman.

"Um, Mick said you were up here grabbing some things for me." She wrung her hands tight like a sponge.

"Yeah, I didn't know what was yours or Angie's, but I figured something was better than nothing. I also grabbed your computer and phone." I pointed to the chair I sat her in last night so she wouldn't cut her feet on the glass we now stood on.

"Thanks. Speaking of phones … " She reached into her pocket and handed me back my phone. "Thanks again for letting me use it today. My folks send their appreciation for keeping me safe."

I gave her a nod like I'd lost all capacity to communicate any other way.

"I may have accidentally come across some things on your phone." She inched closer to me.

My heart plunged to my stomach like a water slide. Shit, did she find my emails proving I was WhoDat, or did she see the porn?

"I … I had no idea you took those photos of me. The one in the jersey, and the night after the party and stuff." She wrapped her arms around her chest as she took a step, closing the distance between us. So much so, the smell of my shampoo in her hair hit me like a crashing wave, sending a spike of adrenaline through me.

"They're my favorite ones." *So lame, Jai. So lame.*

"Jai … " A splash of yellow and orange from the setting sun hit the top of her hair, draping the side of her face in a fiery hue. I burned just as hot looking at her.

"I'm trying so hard, Cat." I clenched a fist at my side.

She bit her lip in that sexy, angsty pout that lit my insides up like a volcano. Just one more kiss. Just one.

I rushed her, pushing her back against the wall as I claimed her lips with my own. Cradling her head with my hands, I put everything into that kiss that I could never say with words. The sexiest moan purred in her throat as she slid her tongue over mine. Her fingertips worked in a fury to rip my shirt from my pants. I grabbed her hands and slammed them against the wall above her head.

She had to listen to what I was trying to tell her with the kiss. Things I couldn't tell her, like I love you. I love you so much it burns inside my heart like an all-consuming fire. Like, I would go to the ends of the Earth to make sure you were happy and safe. I will always protect you and be there for you in my heart. Even if I can't in person.

She relaxed beneath me as she let go and allowed me to speak to her in a language only she and I could understand. I released her hands and slid mine down the sides of her face, holding onto her one last time. As I tried to ease back from her lips, she lunged at my mouth and pulled me back.

She flipped me around and pressed me against the wall, running her hands the length of my torso. Before I could stop her, she ripped my shirt over my head and tossed it to the floor.

Pressing her lips to my chest, she kissed her way down to my jeans unleashing a shiver that tore down my spine.

"Cat," I said. "If we do this again, it'll only be more painful to say goodbye."

"I know," she choked out and threw herself at my chest, wrapping her arms so tight around it knocked the wind out of me.

Curling my fingers into her hair, I buried my face against her neck drinking in her scent one last time. "Cat, I lo—"

"—No. Don't you dare. Don't you even say it and then leave me. Please don't." Sobs ripped from her chest as she wept against me, drenching my skin in tears.

Clenching my jaw, I fought to hold back my own. "I don't have any condoms on me."

"I'm on the pill." She pulled back and locked onto my eyes.

I forced the words out of my mouth, regretting them as each one left my lips. "This is the last time we can ever do this."

I stared into her bloodshot eyes as the sunlight faded into the horizon, painting the sky a brilliant pink and orange, like melted Popsicles. I wanted to take her picture with that as the background. But no more pictures of her. One last time together would be my only reminder.

I tore the glass covered blankets from her bunk, picked her up, and threw her on the bed. We shred each other's clothes like we couldn't get them off fast enough. Sliding a hand between her thighs, my fingers swam in her arousal. Damn, no other woman had ever been so hot for me. A loud groan ripped from her lips as I ran my fingers the length of her. Each moan rang out louder through the room, and a rush of warmth and energy flooded my stomach. She wasn't even trying to be quiet, taking the moment for what it was ... our last time together.

Nothing prepared me for how incredible it was to be inside her unsheathed. I slid in and nearly came in one thrust. An unexpected growl rumbled in my chest like a hungry bear. It shocked the hell out of me. Sex with her was unlike anything else in the world. Like our bodies were meant to fit together, missing pieces.

Every movement I lost myself further in her. She needed me. No one had ever needed me. And I needed her.

As she tightened around me, I gasped so hard it made me dizzy. I dove against her neck, sucking her flesh into my mouth. Something snapped in me. I gripped the top of her head, curling my fingers in her hair right to her scalp trying to hang on as I drove into her like a wild animal. Her body writhed beneath me, arching up to meet my thrusts.

"Jaidev." My name came out of her mouth like a prayer, gasping and breathless. She used my full name and nothing sounded so good to me surrounded by her moans of pleasure, knowing it was me giving it to her.

Sharp nails gripped my back as she shuddered beneath me, and I never came so hard in my life. My own orgasm ripped through my body like the tornado from last night, ravaging every muscle with a spasm of ecstasy. I collapsed against her chest, fighting for breath. She wrapped me in her arms, and I dotted her head with kisses until my lips hurt.

She claimed my soul as we shared one last kiss, and I struggled to burn into my memory the feel of her heated, soft body beneath me. From that moment on I'd be an empty shell, because Catherine Marek had my heart completely. And I'd never be the same ever again.

CHAPTER 21

CAT

Our walk back to Jai's house took every ounce of my strength. Emotional exhaustion made not only my head and heart ache, but my body. Or it could have been the sex. I didn't think it possible to be even better than our first time, but Jai turned all kinds of alpha on me. Like he claimed me, marking his territory. If only he could do that and stand up to his parents.

Jai's fingers gripped mine, as if I'd disappear if he let go. "Let's just run away. We don't have to go back. We can go to Wisconsin, where your family is."

I jerked him to a stop, and he turned to face me. "I would love to run away with you. But I also don't want to become your regret. If we run, you'ill lose your family forever, Jai. I will never make you choose between me and them."

"My regret will be *not* running and having a future with you." He slid a hand along my cheek, brushing a thumb in soft wisps against my skin.

"What if we run away, and then we find out that whatever this incredible thing is between us was only the result of us not being able to be together. That once we are able to, that the spark will fade. That you'll wish you'd never left your family for a girl." Waves of nausea pitched and rolled in the storm of worry in my stomach.

Jai shook his head. "So, you're gonna play the 'what if' game now? That's a bunch of shit, Cat, and you know it. You're starting to sound like my mother. What if we run away, and we live a long happy life together, make lots of babies, make lots of memories, and make our dreams come true? Why do you choose to see the bad and not the good side of the coin?"

I shook my head. Cramps knotted my curling toes in my shoes, and my nails bit into the fleshy palms of my hands as I tried to fight back the tears. "Because I'll never be good enough for you. I saw the look in your parent's eyes when they looked at me."

The hard lines around his eyes softened. "Why can't you believe in yourself? I tried to show that to you the other day, with those photographs. I see what's inside of you, what you try to hide from the world. Is my belief in you—in us—not enough? I don't want to lose you, Cat."

"You won't lose me. We can still remain friends. I'll always be your friend." The words left a bitter taste on my tongue. Kanti all but begged me to remain in Jai's life, but the look from his parents earlier in the day told me they would have something to say about it.

"So, now *you're* friend zoning *me*?" He hitched a shoulder and dropped my hand from his grasp, shaking his head. My heart snapped in two at the anger in his eyes. "You must not feel like I do then. Or you wouldn't even doubt my feelings for you. You doubt what I'd do to keep us together. Here I thought, after that kiss, after I rescued you, after we made love like I've never made love in my life, that you would believe in us."

If only he could feel the piercing of my heart as I tried to make myself believe my own words. "What about finishing school? Your photojournalism career? You're a semester away from graduating, you're gonna give that up, too?"

Hard lines darkened his face. "That dream's gone no matter which path I choose. If I marry Kanti, my father won't allow me to continue with photography."

Running away scared the shit out of me. Part fear, part excitement. But his mother's words hung over my head like an anvil, and the desperation on her face replayed in my head as she begged me stay out of her son's life. Jai had no idea she cornered me earlier in the afternoon when Angie and I got back from the store.

Now the moment of truth came. Could I give him up so he could have a good life, keep his parents, keep his cultural values in place, and retain the honor of his family? Or make him give that up for us maybe having a life together. His family loved him, that was clear. And I truly believed in their heart of hearts they thought they were doing the best thing for him.

"I . . . I . . . " Tremors ricocheted through my hands, up along my arms, and spread like a venom through my body. "I can't. I . . . just can't."

The pain in his eyes stabbed at my heart, and my chest caved. He turned and walked into the house. All the air whooshed from my lungs, and I collapsed in a heap in the grass, clutching my chest like someone just sliced me open. Sobs ripped through my body, and I cried until I had nothing left. I'd never hurt so bad in my entire life. Like my soul was just been ripped from me.

Angie tore out of the house and dropped to her knees at my side. "Cat, what the ever loving hell? What did he do?"

"It was me." The words choked on my tears. "I just gave up the love of my life."

Angie collected me in her arms and rocked me, brushing a hand through my hair. "Oh, sweetie."

Mick followed her out. "Here, let's get her inside." He scooped me into his arms and carried me up to Jai's room.

They'd set up an air mattress on the floor for Angie, assuming I'd want Jai's bed. But the room swallowed me, drowning me in memories that continued to stab at my heart. I couldn't stay there. I couldn't take any more of this pain. It felt like death.

"You need some distraction. Why don't you get online and talk to that Doctor Who guy. Take your mind off things." Angie hunkered down on the air mattress, clasping her arms around her knees.

"I don't feel like talking to anyone right now." As I wiped my face with my sleeve, my eyes focused in on Jai's camera sitting on his desk.

Brushing a finger over it, I accidentally turned it on. Up

popped the folder of pics from our photo shoot. My heart hammered to a hum as I stared at all the pictures. Tears once again filled my eyes and leaked over my cheeks in an overflowing stream. Flutters ransacked my belly, swishing over the waves of nausea and worry.

Jai was my perfect man. My sexy geek, amazing lover, brave rescuer, honest friend, and my eye opener. He made me see things from a different angle, including myself. I wiped away the tears, and a giant smile plastered itself all over my face.

That was it. I wasn't going down without a fight. Culture be damned. They may not believe in romantic marriage, but I sure as hell believed in happy endings. Time to tap into my geeky side and show them my superpower.

Love.

"Ang, I need your help." Ideas swarmed my head. I knew just how to prove to Jai that I loved him, while helping him prove himself to his family at the same time.

As I flipped through the pictures, the shots he took of the tornado aftermath showed up. He not only showed the horrific physical devastation, but the emotional as well. Every picture told its own story. Jai captured the very essence of a person with his shots, zeroing in on their eyes, their expressions.

Grief erupted through tears as people stared at the wreckage of their destroyed homes and buildings. Relief flooded through tight embraces as mothers, daughters, sisters, brothers clung to each other just happy to be alive. They weren't just victims. He showed them as survivors.

He made me a survivor.

I ran to his closet and combed through all his clothes, finally deciding on one as I pulled it off the hanger and rolled it up into my duffle bag.

"Okay, you're running around here like a mad scientist. What's going on in that head of yours?" Angie arched a brow. "I haven't seen you this determined since you told me about Project Panty Drop."

"This one I have much more invested in. Operation Save Superman is now in effect." I bit back the smile creasing my lips as a knock hit the door.

"Come in," Angie said.

Mick peeked his head in. "Just checking on you guys."

Angie walked over and wrapped her arms around him. "We're okay. And, I think Cat's got something up her sleeve now."

"Good. Truthfully, Jai asked me to make sure Cat was okay." He nodded my direction. "He may have been a dick, but only because he's in pain. Don't hate him."

My heart somersaulted in my stomach. Even though he was beyond pissed off at me, he still cared. Because he was Jai. "I'm better now. Thanks. I know he's hurting as much as I am. I don't blame him." I forced a smile.

"Good. I know this is hard on both of you. I've known Jai for a really long time. I've never seen him this tore up. It sucks balls that you guys have to be ripped apart like this. So, just wanna say I'm sorry." Mick placed a hand on my shoulder before pulling Angie to him, placing a soft kiss on her mouth.

I used to take things like that for granted. Being able to love freely, express that love in front of God and country. When that's stripped from you it can go one of two ways; it makes you a fighter and compassionate to the struggle of others, or it turns you into a cold, harsh person, shutting off from the world in order to deal with pain. Like Jai's mom. She was just the result of the world she lived in. I didn't agree with it, but I understood it to an extent.

But this was my world. My life. My love. I decided to choose the path of a fighter. "Mick, can you do me a favor? You're in graphic arts, right?"

He nodded. "What do you need?"

"Can you help me get some flyers printed up for the fundraiser? But we have to make sure Jai never sees them. It's part of the surprise I've got planned for his birthday portion of the party."

Mick's brow knit together. "Should I be scared by what you've got planned? I've seen you in action with the sociology paper."

"Only if you're not in it to help Jai. He's my main focus. It's time to bring some things to light."

"You know I'm all in." Mick folded his arms.

"Good, then I need to get hold of a sound system, projectors, and screens." Whipping out my notebook, I made a list and flow charts of how the evening would go down. "Oh, and on Friday night, you need to make sure Jai wears this." I handed him Jai's Superman t-shirt.

Mick stared at the shirt in my hands. "His mom's making him wear some suit or something. She still wants it a formal party."

"Even better. Make sure he wears it *under* the suit then." A wide smile brimmed my lips. "And you don't breathe a word of this to Jai. At. All. I want him to still be mad at me. He needs to have no idea of what's going on. If he gives any indication there's something planned at the party, his mom will pick up on it and try and stop me."

"You're kind of scary when you're determined." Mick took the shirt with some reluctance.

"I know, right? I just told her that," Angie said.

Rolling my eyes, I curled up on Jai's bed. The smell of his cologne hit me like a ton of bricks and it only reassured me I had to do this. My plan may go down in flames. But at least I'd go down fighting.

CHAPTER 22

JAI

I managed to avoid Cat for the next couple of days. My head and heart warred with each other. The words she said didn't match up with her actions. How could she tell me in one breath that she didn't love me enough to think we could make something of a relationship together, yet in the next minute collapse in tears on the lawn like her world crashed around her?

I admit it, I was a total and complete prick. I left her there after she jabbed a giant fire poker in my heart and skewered my soul like one of my kabobs. Even I couldn't remain that heartless though, and sent Angie and Mick after her. What she didn't know, I watched in the shadows as they got her to my room safely.

Mick even did me a solid and went to check on her later that night after I badgered him enough. Yeah, she may not love me like I loved her, but I would never give up on her like she gave up on me.

Maybe Mom was right about the arranged marriage. When emotions got involved it led to a trail of bad decisions and heartbreak. I understood now the concept of making it a partnership not a relationship. Kanti and I would make an epic partnership. I'd just be celibate the rest of my life and have calluses on my hands. But, better than having your heart ripped from your chest, stomped on with stilettos, and left to rot.

"So, Angie got word this morning they're moving the girls from San Jac Hall to a motel until the reconstruction is done. As of tonight," Mick said, coming back in from a shower with Angie.

That was their latest thing, shower sex. Mick's bedroom happened to be right next to the bathroom, and I got an earful every morning and night. They really liked being clean. And the small fact that Angie didn't have a room and I bunked with Mick, left little privacy. Get it in where you can, I guess.

Every damn time it made me think back to my almost shower sex with Cat. Damn, I'd been so very close to taking her in the shower after I washed her hair. But I hadn't planned on giving in to my lust for her at all, let alone wanting the first time to be in the tiny shower. I managed to wait a full five seconds after I got her back to my room.

There were moments I wished she'd never even come into my life. Like it would have been better to just never have known her than feel this pain. But I thought back to her smile, how she made me come alive, how remarkable of a person she really was. My perfect match completely. She had to walk into my life right before I had to get married. How cruel fate is.

"Did you hear me?" Mick said.

"Huh?" I shook my head. "Oh, right. Yeah. Cool, I get my room back. I'll be out of yours so you can stop cleaning your dick twice a day."

Mick chuckled. "Sorry. We try to keep it down, but damn, Angie's a moaner."

Angie's moans annoyed the piss out of me. Cat's moans took me to another world and set me on fire.

"You gonna go say goodbye to her?" Mick leaned against the door.

I quirked a brow. "To Angie?"

"No, you douche. To Cat," Mick said.

"We already said our goodbyes. There's no need." But my heart sank at the thought of her no longer being down the hall from me.

Even though we'd managed not to talk for the last couple days, I'd sneak looks at her, hiding in my own damn house. My heart still twinged at the sight of her. We were far from over. But I couldn't make her love me enough to make a go of it, so what was the point? I had no time to continue to try and convince her. In a couple weeks, I'd be on a plane to India and getting married.

"I don't think she's coming to the party tonight. From what Angie said, they're just gonna head to the motel and get out of our hair." Mick got changed and did a double check in the mirror to make sure every last dark-blond hair remained in place. Dude just needed to use product and get over it.

"It'll be for the best anyway. I'm sure my folks would make it awkward. And there's mainly just a bunch of my cousins and parents' friends coming. I haven't even heard anyone mention the fundraiser on campus. I've tried to talk a few people into coming, but everyone's so busy with the cleanup no one has time."

Just another stab in the gut. No one wanted to help raise funds for the victims of the tornado, or celebrate my birthday. Turning twenty-two sucked major balls no matter how I looked at it.

Another rap on the door pulled me from my vicious circle of thoughts. "Jaidev, are you in there?" My mother's voice, which used to soothe me, now grated my nerves worse than nails on a chalk board.

"Yes," I said just above a whisper.

"I have your suit from Chandar. Open your door." Another rap rang out from behind the door. Patience was never her strong suit.

"Dude, better let her in before she huffs and puffs and blows it down. We can't afford to fix anything else in this place." Mick laughed and thumbed over his shoulder at the door.

My eyes rolled so hard I nearly somersaulted off the bed. "You used to be my friend."

"Oh believe me. I still am." Mick slapped a hand on my shoulder. "You're going to go have a good time tonight. I guarantee it."

I arched a brow. Unless he filled the place with strippers and sent my parents to India without me, I doubted it.

My mother burst through the door before I could even open it, and Mick dove into his closet, trying to get his last leg into a pair of jeans.

"Mom, you can't just barge in here. This is Mick's room." I took the stupid suit from her and hung it on the back of the door.

"You need to get ready. Your cousins are here. And Kanti, she looks stunning." Mother unwrapped the suit from the garment bag.

"I'll be down in a minute." I huffed.

Mother cupped my cheek, then gave it a little pat. "Smile, Jaidev. It is the celebration of the day of your birth. Be happy."

I slid off my t-shirt. "Don't feel much like celebrating."

"This Catherine person. She does love you. She did as I asked and respected my wishes. That shows honor to your family. Though I know you cannot be with her, I'm proud you made the choice to love someone who cares enough about you and your family to let you go." Mother reached for the door, but I clasped my hand over her wrist.

"What?" My eyes widened. The knots in my stomach tugged tighter as I processed her words. "Did you say something to Cat?" I spun her around and looked into her eyes. The eyes never lie, which is why I most often photographed them. "Did you tell her to let me go?"

"It was for the best, Jaidev. You'll see that in time." Giving my hand a pat, she shut the door.

The room spun around me. The knots in my stomach worked their way up to my throat and wedged themselves there. Here I blamed Cat for giving up on us, and she was doing what my mother asked of her, because she loved me. I was such an utter asshole to her, left her convulsing in sobs on the front lawn as she let me go at my mother's request. She loved me enough to let me go.

I hit the floor with a thud and slammed my back against Mick's bed. Running my hands through my hair, I tugged at the ends until pain ripped through my scalp. How stupid could I be? I was so torn up over my own hurt, I never saw through to Cat's. I never looked her in the eyes and saw what she was really doing.

Now I'd never get to say goodbye. She was gone.

"Dude, I'm so sorry. I had no idea your mom told Cat to leave. If I'd known I would have told you." Mick gave my shoulder a squeeze as he dropped to a squat.

"I know," I choked out. "I fucked up bad, man. Really bad. Cat tried so hard that night, wanting to remain friends. I ran out on her when she needed me the most. She deserves better than me. Maybe my mother's right. This is for the best. Marrying Kanti, I can't fuck up anyone else's life."

"Jai, man, you can't think like that. What your mom did was way wrong. It was yours and Cat's business to take care of, not hers. I'm sure if you talk to Cat … "

I shook my head. "No. I can't put her through anymore. She's been through so much in the last couple of weeks. If I try and talk to her now, it'll only bring her more pain, more hurt. What she needs is healing, and to stay far the hell away from me."

"Well, why not go downstairs, get piss drunk and enjoy your birthday party as a free man." He offered me a hand and yanked me up from the floor.

"Piss drunk, yes. Enjoy myself? No." I blew out a hard breath and slipped on the white button down shirt.

"Hey, put this on." He tossed me my Superman t-shirt.

"Are you insane? My mom will flip her shit if I come down in that. I really don't want to deal with any more crap right now. I just want to go down there, get drunk, and pass the fuck out."

"How about wear it under your suit? Just like Superman. Kind of an ode to Cat. She was into all that geeky shit you are, right?"

I stared at the shirt, thinking back to the night she saw the comic books on my floor. Even I didn't get as excited as she did when she found my rare Fantastic Four comic from 1961. The look on her face ranged somewhere between heart attack and orgasm.

Nodding, I took the shirt and slid it over my head.

"Good deal. I'll meet you downstairs." Mick tossed a salute and left.

One last night to remember her. Then tomorrow, I'd begin the process of trying to forget her.

I gave myself a once over in the mirror. The dark gray suit didn't look half bad. Though my hair had a mind of its own and I looked like Hindu Elvis. Shoving my fingers through the mess, I worked it down and went for the messed up after-sex look. Then I remembered Cat's after-sex hair, and regret punched me at the thought of what my mother and I did to her.

I needed a beer, now, or I'd never make it through this night. Jogging down the stairs, I jerked to a stop as I hit the bottom. The common room looked like Shiva threw up in my house. The Indian restaurant, not the god. Curry and Masala assaulted my senses. Table upon table took up every last bit of space between the large living room and kitchen. My parents spared no expense on the food. We wouldn't run out anytime soon.

"Jaidev," someone called out in the sea of people gathering around all the food.

It would take a good twenty minutes just to get to the back door. And of course, that's where the beer was.

"Cousin," someone shouted again, and a face stood out from the crowd.

"Vijay." I threw my arms around my cousin, giving him a manly slap on the back.

"Long time, man." He shook my hand and shoved a samosa in his mouth with the other.

"Yeah. Thanks for coming," I said, but a blast of music swallowed my voice.

When I didn't think it could get worse, my mother decided the soundtracks from every Bollywood movie in the last ten years would complement the evening nicely. If I didn't get a beer in me I'd end up going to jail for beating someone with a pan of Tikka Masala.

By the time I made it to the kitchen I hated the sound of my own name. Every single member of my family not living in India stood in between me and my beer. Not a single student on campus showed up, sans the ones already living in the house.

Shoving myself through my swarm of lineage, I finally found the back door. Mick slid out of nowhere and blocked my exit.

"So, enjoying your party?" he asked.

"Seriously? I've been trying to get to a beer for half an hour. And you're the last person in my way. So please let me out the door so I don't choose you to be the one I hulk-out on. You're the only one not related to me in here right now, and the only one I really don't want to have to shiv."

If nothing else, I had at least a six-pack in my mini fridge in my room. Now that Cat had left, I could make my way back upstairs and just drink enough to get somewhat of a buzz and maybe fall asleep.

"Got your beer right here." Mick held up a cold Shiner and nothing looked so good in my life.

"I could kiss you, man." I grabbed the beer, popped the top, and slammed the shit out of it.

"Please don't. I'm not ready to take our relationship to the next level," Mick said with a laugh.

As the last of the nectar of the gods slid down my throat, I relished the silence, as no one else had called my name in at least five minutes.

"You hanging in there?" Mick chugged a beer himself.

I gave a nod, chucking the bottle in the recycle bin by the back door. "Gonna give it another five minutes and then just go to my room and call it. I made an appearance, enough for people to show proof in pictures I was here. In my mother's suit."

Mick handed me another beer. "Well that would kind of suck, you'll miss the entertainment."

"Entertainment?" I cocked my head. "You totally didn't hire strippers with my parents here, did you?"

"Oh, I think you'll enjoy this so much more." Mick placed an arm around my shoulder and guided me through the back door.

A blanket of blackness shrouded the backyard. Mick walked me out a few feet and stopped.

"What happened to all the yard lights?" I asked, doing my best to make out figures moving through the cover of darkness.

"Stand here," Mick said.

I looked around and a tingle wove its way up my spine. What the hell?

Strings of white lights clicked on along the perimeter of the yard, hung from paper lanterns drooping and swaying along the trees and bushes. Another set of lights clicked on, focusing on six large screens standing at various intervals in a semi-circle around the edges of the yard.

I cocked a brow. "What's going on?"

My family filtered outside from the house. More lights clicked on in the center of the yard where a raised platform stood. From the shadows, people crept into the light. Faces from all around campus came into focus, some I recognized, some I knew only in passing. And every single one of them had on some kind of geeky shirt, from Doctor Who to Superheroes.

I took a hard swallow as more and more people filed in from the edges not lit up by the white lanterns. Hundreds of people filled the yard, weaving in between the large screens, working their way in front of me and the large platform in the middle.

I watched the bewildered expressions as my family crowded around me in the remainder of the yard, especially my parents, who's confusion matched my own. "Okay, Mick. Seriously, what the hell's going on?"

CHAPTER 23

CAT

Sweat beaded my brow, and I hadn't even made it on stage yet. My heart lurched into my throat, hammering so hard I probably looked like a croaking frog. Tingles flooded my arms and legs, as jittery nerves took over my last coherent thoughts.

Please don't let my limbs give out on me!

"What's he saying?" I asked, to anyone who would listen.

"I can't hear him, we're all back here with you silly," Angie said from somewhere behind me. In the dark, all the muffled noise made it hard to pinpoint anyone's location. "But the look on his face is priceless. He's kind of sporting the WTF highbrow."

My heart plunged from my throat to my stomach on butterfly wings.

I hadn't stepped foot on stage since I was twelve. After the accident and I lost my hearing, most of that came to an end. I dove inward, instead of striving to continue outward. Thus, I developed my inner geek. If it weren't for Doctor Who, comic books, and sci-fi, I may not have survived the change from normal child to a disabled one.

Sure, I knew there were kids far worse off than me. But my world still changed entirely, and to a twelve-year-old it was devastating. I stopped performing, for fear I would never be able to keep in tune or a beat. My favorite thing in the world to do became my worst fear. That fear resulted in me choosing audiology as a career. I wanted to help kids avoid my depression and shame as a child.

But tonight would change that. Tonight I would bring all of me back to fight for Jai. Even if nothing changed the situation as a result, he'd know I'd given him everything. Somehow I hoped this made up for the mistake in listening to his mother and not him.

Kanti worked on getting me into the last piece of the lehenga she loaned me. A gold paisley pattern accented the long white umbrella-cut skirt that flowed almost to the floor. The gold and white short-sleeve top fit snug against my torso, leaving just enough of my stomach exposed that goosebumps fired along my skin as the crisp breeze blew. She wrapped a gold and white scarf along my neck, the ends of which draped down my back.

We covered up another outfit hiding beneath. But at the end of the song I'd still have to change into one last piece of my costume. Kanti's skill at hiding clothing registered at epic levels. Between her helping me with lyrics and Angie choreographing us, we worked the last couple of days until our bodies were numb.

"God, I feel like I'm going to pass out." I wiped a hand across my forehead beading with sweat from nerves.

"You will be fine." Kanti smiled and tugged at my long ponytail. "You nailed it in practice repeatedly. You could do this in your sleep now. Why you ever gave up dancing and singing is beyond me. You have a gift for it." She swatted at my hand. "Don't touch your face, you'll smudge your eyeliner."

Kanti had spent the last thirty minutes transforming me from geek chic to exotic Bollywood model by sheer magic. I was fully convinced she had some hidden superpower. Shaking my head, I swallowed back the bubble of bile working its way up my throat.

Please don't let me puke. Please don't let me puke.

I hadn't been this frightened since my first time on stage.

"Okay, we're ready," Mick said, panting as he got in position.

I blew out a breath, shook my hands out, and got in position on the stage under the cover of the dark. Now or never.

Pounding beats from the bass drum cued us. We set out on stage, clapping to the beat as the song Jai Ho, from the Slumdog Millionaire soundtrack started. Time to channel my inner Pussycat Doll.

I slid on stage and the song swept me away as I sang my heart out, becoming someone else entirely. Even though the music somewhat distorted in my ears, Kanti and Angie worked to get my timing down so I used the drumming base to dance to. No longer Catherine or even Cat, I turned into my own superhero trying to win back the man of my dreams.

Hips swaying, Angie, Maya, Kanti, and I moved across the stage, doing our best to look sexy. Well, I tried. Angie, Maya and Kanti had it spades.

I hit center stage and caught sight of Jai across the sea of people as one of the spotlights we'd set up hit him. The look on his face sent a pulse of adrenaline to my heart as we locked eyes, professing my love for him through the song. Bewilderment, fascination, perhaps even lust flickered in his eyes, and he never took them off me. I fought the giggle welling in my belly as his mouth popped open as the realization hit that it was me under the exotic makeup and Indian garb. It drove me onward, and I cranked it up a notch, throwing extra sway in my hips.

Someone tried to talk to him and he held up a hand, never taking his attention off me. His eyes narrowed as he fought back a smile with twitching lips. I had no idea where his parents were. Probably appalled somewhere in a corner plotting my demise. I didn't care. The look on Jai's face made every minute of this worthwhile.

The last beat of the song hit, we all bowed in our Namaste pose as the lights clicked off and blackness swallowed us. Kanti and Maya rushed to get me out of the lehenga. Beneath it I already had on jeans, but Angie came up from behind me and slid a t-shirt over my head.

As the applause, catcalls, and cheers died, I clicked my mic back on and but remained off stage.

"Ladies and gentlemen, thank you all for coming this evening." The music behind me switched to heavy techno-symphonic as the screens lit up all around the yard. Pics scrolled through on every one of them, detailing the wreckage from the storm. All of them Jai's pictures. Every one of them gut wrenching and real.

Jai stalked his way to the stage, but jerked to a stop as he caught sight of the pictures on all the screens. He spun around in a slow circle, mouth open and wide-eyed.

"Tonight we are here for several reasons. One of them is to help raise funds for the victims of the EF-2 tornado that struck UT-Austin's campus last week. As you can see by the pictures of the aftermath, some of these lives will never be the same."

The sea of faces hung on my words as every last one of them stared at all six screens spread through the yard.

"If you would like to make a donation, Kanti, Maya, and Angie will be walking through the crowd to make it easy for you to help change someone's life with something as simple as a dollar."

People fumbled into their wallets as the girls left the stage with buckets to start the collection.

"But tonight, we also have a celebration. We celebrate and honor the survivors. We celebrate life. And one very special birthday in the crowd."

Whoops and hollers filled the air as a mass of guys yelled out Jai's name.

"But also, it's about celebrating those unsung heroes in the crowd. Which is why you were asked to wear your favorite superhero shirt or cosplay tonight."

Streams of people stepped on to the stage dressed from Wonder Woman to Batman and everything in between.

"I asked you all to come as your favorite superhero for a reason. I know many of you were victims of this storm, as was I. And because of one hero, I'm here standing before you. And I, too, dressed up as my favorite superhero."

I stepped into the spotlight wearing Jai's Batman shirt and jeans. Slipping Jai's glasses along my nose, I prayed he'd forgive me that I stole them from his room. His mouth twitched as it popped open again, and he shook his head.

"I'm dressed up to honor my hero, Jaidev Sankar, who's rescued me on several occasions. Not only from the tornado, but from storms in my personal life. He showed me my true self. He showed me how to love. He showed me I can be loved."

Blood thrummed in my veins as my heart hammered so hard and fast I thought it would leap from my chest. Jai plunged into the crowd, fighting to make his way to the stage. I lost him in the mass of people.

"Mr. and Mrs. Sankar, I know you're out there somewhere. And I want you to know … " I sucked in a deep breath as I fought back the whirlwind of emotions pile-driving me. *No tears. No tears. Make it through with no tears.* "I want you to know that I am absolutely, completely, ridiculously in love with your son, Jaidev. And I will never give up on him. I will never give up on us."

I tried to find Jai somewhere in the sea of people crowding the stage. My head swam with dizziness as I desperately tried to locate him. Maybe it was too much. Maybe he got embarrassed and ran.

Someone spun me around, and before I could see who it was, a mouth claimed mine and dipped me into a set of arms. As soon as his cologne hit my nose I knew it was Jai. His tongue passed my lips and danced with mine with furious passion. I dropped the mic to the floor and wrapped my arms around him so tight my hands cramped.

She never tasted so good. I didn't care who the hell was in the audience watching me make out with my girlfriend on stage. I didn't care that my parents were probably having heart attacks somewhere in my back yard. All I cared about was giving back to Cat what she just gave to me.

No one in my life had ever done anything so spectacular, so outrageous and amazing for me. It all made sense now. I pulled her back to her feet, even though all I wanted to do was kiss her for the rest of my natural life. However short that may be once my parents made their way to the stage.

Her hands clawed at my chest, grabbing hold of my white button-down shirt. She ripped it open, popping buttons into the air. Our lips parted, and she spun me around revealing the Superman t-shirt under my suit. The crowd roared its approval. I could only imagine how it must have been for Cat. She shied away with a laugh as the audience turned into a mosh pit of excitement cheering us on to kiss again.

Who was I to deny them? Sliding my hand along her waist, I yanked her back to me and cradled her head with my other hand. As my lips met hers, a pair of hands grabbed me from behind and jerked me away from her. They spun me around, and I came face to face with my father.

Shit.

My mother grabbed Cat by the shoulders. "I thought you were going to honor our agreement. You claim to love Jai, yet you continue trying to ruin his life with this … this outrageousness?"

"Mr. and Mrs. Sankar, I understand wanting to keep a cultural identity. To maintain certain customs, continue your ethnicity. But people evolve, ideas evolve. How is forcing a person to marry someone they don't love a good thing? How is stopping someone from living their dream going to help them be a better person?"

Cat's words shocked me, and my parents no less. My parents' faces hardened like stone, though my mother's eyes stone-like glare cracked as they glassed over for a moment.

"I love Jai. With everything in me. I will fight for him, with him, help him reach his dreams. Look." She pointed to the screens surrounding us. "Just look at the good he can do. Look at those faces. Emotions caught in time and space. He doesn't take pictures. He lets us see people's souls. He gives light to darkness, voices to those who can't speak, and a window to those who can't see. How is that not just as important in life as a doctor, a lawyer, a business owner?"

She turned to my father and he took a step back, glancing between Cat, then at the screens behind her. "Mr. Sankar, there is no shame in being proud of your son who provides beauty to the world, who helps others. He is one of the most selfless people I've ever met. From the moment I met him, he's always been doing something for someone else. There are many ways of measuring honor. Jai exceeds them all."

I gripped Cat's hand as I fought the tears flooding my eyes. A tornado of emotions ripped through me and words lodged in my throat. Closing my eyes, I sucked in a deep breath. "I don't want to marry Kanti. I'm in love with Cat. If she hasn't just proven what a worthy partner in life she would be, then there's nothing else we can do."

"You're right, there's nothing else you can do," my father said, and beckoned for Kanti's father and a couple of my cousins to come to the stage.

"Anil, please." My mother addressed my father with a shake of her head. Worry flashed through the glassy pools waiting to fall from her eyes.

My father's stern eyes burned towards my mother.

Tears claimed my mother's face as she clasped Cat's hand and squeezed. "I'm so sorry. You will make another man an honorable wife someday. Thank you for what you tried to do for my son."

My father gripped my shoulders and ushered me off stage. I jerked back and tried to run back to Cat, but he grabbed me by my waist and shoved me down the stairs. "Cat!" I yelled out.

Cat dove after me and clasped my hand. "Jaidev!" Tears streamed down her cheeks.

My mother grabbed her by the crook of her elbow and held her back. "There's nothing more you can do."

"But there's something I can," Kanti said from behind me as she grabbed the mic from the floor. "Mom, dad … I'm gay. And Maya and I are in love. I don't want to marry Jaidev."

Maya stepped from the shadows and clasped hands with her. Kanti pulled her close and pressed her lips to Maya's mouth in a delicate, loving kiss.

Kanti's mother slapped a hand to her face and fainted in my mother's arms. My stomach plunged to my toes as I watched everything in my entire world crumble around me. For one pure blissful second, I had it all. Now, I was pretty sure we'd be sent back to India in chains, never to be seen or heard from again.

Cat's tears streamed down her face as she hugged Maya and Kanti, then turned to look at me, still in the clutches of my father.

"You didn't have to do that Kanti," I shouted, and a tear slipped from my own eye and plunged to the grass.

"Yes, Jaidev, I did. Not only for you, but for me. For Maya. I needed to for a long while." Kanti slipped her arm around Maya.

"Jaidev, you knew about this?" My mother yelled to me.

"Wasn't my secret to tell," I said, shirking from my father's grip.

"We'll discuss this matter in private," my father said, clamping down on my arm so tight I thought his fingers would bore right into my flesh.

I knew after tonight I'd never see Cat ever again. Or any one of my friends here. Mick stepped forward with clamped fists, but I held a hand up and shook my head. We'd made enough of a scene. I didn't want anyone else involved.

"Cat," I yelled her name over my shoulder as I reached the grass at the bottom of the stage. She dove to her knees and held out a hand to me. I reached for it, but my father forced my wrist down. "Thank you. For everything. I will always, always remember you. You have my heart forever."

Mascara and eyeliner ran down her cheeks, as she mouthed I love you.

That moment in time played over in my head forever.

CHAPTER 24

CAT

Finals proved to be harder to get through than I ever imagined. Part of me just didn't care anymore. I somehow managed to go through the motions; getting up, showering, eating. But everything lacked purpose as I contemplated life. A week had gone by since Jai's birthday, and no one had seen or heard from him. Not even Mick. All we knew was they'd taken Jai straight back to Houston with them, along with Kanti.

I launched my bags on my bed and collapsed in a heap. There comes a point in the grieving process where you can't even cry anymore. In seven days I'd run the gamut of hurt, anger, revenge, hurt some more, last pinch of hope, and finally to acceptance.

Angie and Mick did me a favor and kept their romantic adventures out of sight. Which meant she spent a lot of time at the house, and less time at our dorm/motel room. The loneliness both helped, and ate at my soul. Too much time to think. Too much time to miss Jai.

Grabbing a beer from the fridge, I sat at my computer desk and opened my laptop. One more thing to do before calling this semester done and heading home for winter break. The more I thought about it, the more I needed to get out of this place for a while. Some time with my family and friends back home would help me heal. Although, when your heart is ripped from your chest, you never really get over that. You just deal with the gaping hole as best you can. Patch by patch, maybe as time went by it would fill up.

I opened up my sociology paper. I had to proof read it one more time before sending it to my professor. With my Project Panty Drop paper down the tubes, I ended up going a different route in the final draft: Love Doesn't Always Conquer All – Western Romance versus The World.

Now that I was an expert on the subject, I wrote it from a frame of reference having been on both sides of the fence. Truth be told, the paper turned out to be therapeutic as I dug deeper into other cultures and their ideas of romantic marriage versus arranged and/or forced marriages, which actually turned out to be two different things.

Some cultures who believed in arranged marriages still allowed the children right of refusal on their mate, at least having a say or being allowed to agree with the arrangement. Others, like Jai's, it became more forced marriage, with little to no say in the process. Where the elders and parents know what's best for the child and make the arrangements with no input at all from the marrying parties.

An eye opening process to me, it unveiled just how lucky we are in our western culture with societal freedoms in our melting pot. Of course, I only felt that way because I've known the freedom to love who I want to love. People in Jai's culture have only ever known it one way, and most go along with it because of that. But having led a more Westernized life here in the states and Britain, Jai suffered more having been caught in between both worlds.

I managed to even incorporate views from those like Kanti, struggling for equal rights in the LGBT community. She had the universe against her as a lesbian being forced into straight marriage. Her struggle perhaps was the worst of all, being taboo and made a criminal because of who she was as a human being and who she loved.

I always knew the struggle was there, but it never affected me first hand. I never really understood the plight. Even as sympathetic as I thought myself to be to the cause. My research paper wouldn't change the world, but it changed mine.

The door creaked open and Angie came in, halfway hooked to Mick's lips. As much as I wanted to roll my eyes, I held it back and concentrated on the work in front of me. It burned my heart that I didn't want to see them together, all happy and lovey dovey. They deserved to be. But it made me miss Jai all that much more. More reason to get out of there and do some emotional healing.

"I promise, it'll only take a minute," Angie said, breaking free from Mick's grasp before turning to me. "Hey, I've been looking all over for you. Why didn't you answer your phone?"

"Sorry, I've been trying to get this stupid paper done. Must not have heard it ring. What's up?"

"Mick's having a kegger for end of the semester, tonight. You wanna go for a little while?" Angie sat on the edge of her bed and brought out the pouty face.

The last place I wanted to be was that house. I'd manage to avoid it for the last week. I didn't think I'd ever be able to go back there and not break down into a blubbering crybaby.

"Naw, thanks for the invite, but I'm gonna take a polite pass. I've got to get this paper done and then see if I can catch an earlier flight back home. I'm not due to fly out 'til tomorrow afternoon, but maybe I can get out on standby or something." I clasped my hands together trying not to think about Jai, or the party, or any memories at all. But just looking at Mick brought everything flooding back, and I bit into my lip fighting tears.

Angie placed a hand on my shoulder. "You want me to stay here with you for a while?"

I shook my head. "You go on ahead. I appreciate you guys laying low with the kissy stuff. But I'm very happy you guys get to make a go of it. From now on, instead of feeling sorry for myself or jealous, I'm going to celebrate you guys."

Mick dropped to a squat and wrapped me in a tight hug. "Thanks for all you did for my best friend. While I never made out with the guy, I'm missing him like hell. So, I kinda know what you're going through."

Nodding, I gave him a tight squeeze. "I can't believe he hasn't been able to contact even you."

"I'm sure they pretty much cut him off from all his bad-decision-making friends. At least in their eyes." He slid next to

Ang on the bed.

I dropped my gaze to my hands in my lap. "I can't stop thinking about Kanti either. I can't believe she had the balls to do that. I wasn't expecting that at all."

"She's amazing. But at least she did it here, and not say, back in India at the wedding reception, ya know? Didn't she say they'd like stick her in jail or some shit? That's totally whack." Angie shook her head.

"I got a text from Maya that said she hadn't heard from Kanti. She's pretty much in the same position as us. Just waiting for some kind of word." I checked my phone again looking for messages I knew wouldn't be there.

"Well, if I ever do hear from him, I'll definitely let you know." Mick stood and held out a hand to Angie. "We should probably head out."

I stood and gave each of them a hug, as I'd probably not see them again until the end of January when the next semester began.

"You guys take care of yourselves. Don't get into any trouble." Giving each as much of a smile as I could muster, I let out a sigh.

"You too, girl." Angie slid a hand through my hair. "Love ya."

"Love ya, too."

I shut the door behind them and slid myself back into my chair. After one more read through, I typed up an email to Professor Wilkinson and hit send. It almost felt like closing a chapter on a book I just wasn't ready to be done with.

I went to shut down my laptop, but my messenger button dinged. Quirking a brow, I clicked it open to find a message from WhoDat. A little quiver danced in my belly. I hadn't talked to him in weeks. Truthfully, I didn't blame him for ignoring me. I kind of dumped on him right before everything blew up with Jai.

WD: Hey, Impossible Girl, you there?

Me: Yeah, was actually just about to shut down. Trying to get to the airport to fly home for winter break.

WD: Oh, well I'm glad I caught you then.

Me: My plane doesn't actually leave until tomorrow. I just wanted to see if I could get out of here earlier. So much has happened in the last couple of weeks. I'm barely holding on as it is, and any more time here than necessary is killing me.

WD: Things not end well with the other guy?

Me: Not at all. It's such a long story, and it sucks so much because we love each other. We actually and truly love each other, and we can't be together. My heart hurts so much, WD. Just when I think I'll make it through, I think of him and break in half all over again. I don't think I'll ever be whole.

WD: I bet he's thinking the same thing as you right now.

Me: I wouldn't know. I haven't heard from him in a week. We were literally ripped apart from each other. I have no idea where he is, what happened, if he's even alive. His parents were so angry. I think I just messed things up even worse trying to win him back. If I could only hear his voice again. Just know he's okay.

WD: Can I try and cheer you up?

Me: I really appreciate the offer, but nothing will cheer me up. And, I don't want to mislead you with anything. I just need to get out of here.

WD: Oh, come on. Humor me. Just one little joke I think you'll get a kick out of.

Not even WD could make me smile at this point. I briefly entertained the thought about faking a power surge and just shutting down my laptop. I had no patience, no will to explain to someone else how nothing in this world could make me whole right now. Everyone who tried just grated my nerves and made me even angrier. I hated that. I hated that I'd turned into this angry, hateful, spiteful person. But anger was the only thing keeping me from completely drowning in my depression.

I let out a frustrated huff and gave in, only because it was WD.

Me: Okay. Fine.

WD: Knock knock.

Me: Who's there?

WD: Me.

A loud rap on the door scared the shit out of me. I whipped around, and my heart took a swan dive to my stomach. What. The. Fuck?

Me: No.

WD: No, you're not going to let me in? Or no, you don't believe it's really me?

Me: Are you insane?

WD: The thought's crossed my mind a lot lately.

Me: You're really here? Outside my door?

WD: Knock knock.

Another loud knock on the door sent flutters to my belly. I swallowed hard and forced a long, slow breath out to clear my head.

Me: Why are you here? Wait, how the hell did you know where to find me?

WD: Well, if you let me in, things will kind of explain themselves.

Me: How do I know you're not some psychotic internet stalker?

WD: Really? Okay, good point. And if it were anyone else but me out here, I'd be telling you to lock the door and call the police. But it's me, Impossible Girl. You know who I am.

Me: No, I don't really. I mean, we've talked for months online, sure. Okay, I even let you into my cyber-panties. Which is crazy in and of itself because I don't even know your name. Or where you live. Or anything about you.

WD: You know more about me than anyone else on the planet, Cat. You always have.

Me: Cat? How the ...

All the air in my lungs stuck at the back of my throat behind a bottle-necked scream. Tremors rocketed through my hands, and I couldn't type anything back to him. I hoped and prayed and cried and screamed inside. My ass sat glued to my chair out of fear. Fear that if I opened that door and it turned out to not be him I would die a thousand deaths after having one last glimmer of hope. My heart wouldn't be able to withstand breaking again.

WD: Cat? Please let me in. I really, really want to kiss you. Okay, look you can have my collector's edition Fantastic Four comic book if you just open the freaking door.

I bolted from my seat and whipped open the door. Jai stood on the other side holding his phone in one hand and a long-stemmed red rose in the other. Without thinking, I flung myself at him like a monkey and his back slammed against the wall.

I crushed my mouth to his, needing to taste him, craving the reassurance that he was there, standing in front of me. Sliding his hands under my ass, he carried me into the room and kicked the door shut behind us with his foot.

Every movement of his tongue against mine sent an orgasmic flutter straight to my nethers. No denying that was Jai. He sat on my bed and I straddled his lap, still attached to his lips. The moment he attempted to break the kiss and come up for air, I lunged at him and claimed them back. Gripping the back of my head like a lifeline, he moaned against my mouth and a flood of warmth hit my belly.

"I take it you missed me," he said, mouthing the words against my lips.

I jerked back, punched his shoulder, then dove back to his mouth and pressed my tongue firm against his. Warm hands ran up my back as he nestled me against his chest. Finally needing air, I eased off him and cupped the sides of his head with my hands.

"Wait a minute, you're WhoDat?" The realization sunk in.

Oh. My. God. The night I showed him my picture, the very one he took, I professed my love for him not knowing it was him. That must have been why he rescued me that night. Giving myself a giant face-palm, I buried my face in his chest. Not once did he say anything. No wonder why it took him so long to respond after seeing my picture.

He just let me babble on about him, to him. A laugh bubbled up in my belly as I realized the absolute ridiculousness of the situation. I broke up with him telling him I was in love with him. I could just picture that smug smile of his as he read it, too.

God, I'm an idiot.

"Um, surprise." His lopsided grin sent my head for a spin.

Resting my hands on his shoulders, I looked him in the eyes. "Why didn't you tell me sooner? Did you know before I sent you the pic?"

Shaking his head, he dropped his gaze to our laps before slowly making his way back to my eyes. "Had no idea until that night. And after you broke up with me by telling me you were in love with me, which was actually pretty damn awesome all things considered, I didn't have the heart to tell you. I'd hurt you enough." He curled his fingers into my back, gripping me tight.

"Are you back just for finals? I assume this is our formal goodbye." The words tumbled out over my trembling lips. "You know what, don't answer. Just kiss me. Just hold me so tight one last time. I want our last memory to be this, not me screaming your name as you're ripped from my arms."

"Cat," he said, stroking the back of my hair.

I kissed my name off his lips and buried it between our tongues. His arms never held me tighter. Warmth tingled through my body as we held one of our wordless conversations. I leaned him back on the bed and draped my body over his, pressing my breasts against his chest.

A low groan rumbled in his throat as he worked his hands from my hair down to the hem of my shirt, slipping heated fingertips along my skin.

"Cat," he moaned into the kiss.

"Don't talk," I mumbled against his mouth.

"Cat." A laugh bubbled up from his throat and tickled my tongue. His strong hands held my head and eased me from his mouth. "As much as I want to do this right now, please let me just say something."

"No. I can't take another goodbye, Jai." I shook my head in his hands, and his fingertips pressed tenderly into my skin.

"What about a hello?" His Adam's apple bounced in his throat. "What if I was here to stay and not going anywhere?"

I jerked up and my hair hung around us like a waterfall as I stared into his eyes. Their deep espresso color held happiness, not sadness.

"What?" I gasped.

"I'm not going anywhere. I'm not marrying Kanti." His lips curled into a smile as he brushed my drooping hair behind my ears.

"What?" I sat up and pressed my palms to his shoulders. "For real? This isn't some kind of joke or dream?"

He laughed. "For real. The wedding's off."

"But how? What? Oh my God!" I lunged at him and covered him in kisses and he rolled me to the side, staring into my eyes.

"Well, a number of things happened this week and everything just snowballed. Kanti and I had very long talks with our families, alone and together. We all agreed in the light of everything that a wedding was just not going to happen. Thanks to you, my parents are easing off the idea of a forced marriage all together. I think my father's still secretly plotting, but my mother, I think she's at least on our side. I had a pretty awesome heart to heart with her, and when it was all said and done, she likes you. While she's still not sold on all these Western ideas, she liked that you fought for me."

I bit my lip, trying to stop a flow of tears welling up.

"And, I like that you fought for me, too." He ran a hand through my hair, sliding it down along my cheek as he pulled me in for a soft kiss. "That was the most amazing night of my life. Well aside from our sex, because there's really nothing that can compare to that."

A giggle burst through my tears, and he gripped my hands, entwining our fingers.

"You made me see a part of myself. You made others see who I am. You even got through to my parents, as much as they didn't want to admit it. You changed things, Cat. You saved me." His own lips trembled, and he sucked in a gasp of air.

"I'd do it all again in a heartbeat." A thump hit my chest as the realization set in that Jai was now officially mine. No Kanti. No parents. No marriage.

Mine.

"I know." He smiled, brushing fingertips along my jawline. "That's why I'm here. I love you, and want to officially ask you to be my girlfriend."

I rolled over on him and swept his lips into a deep kiss. My fingers sifted through his hair as I gave him my answer. My boyfriend. My Jai.

"Was that a yes?" He slid his hands to my waist. "I'm pretty sure that was a yes, but I kinda wanna hear you say it."

"Yes!" It came out in more of a giggle than an actual word. "So. Much. Yes."

He rolled me over and stared down into my eyes. "You know, we had our first fight a week ago, I think it's time we had make-up sex."

"After you bring me my collector's edition Fantastic Four comic." I winked.

With a roll of his eyes, he buried me in kisses.

THE END

MORE BOOKS BY WREN MICHAELS:

VEXED

Vodou stole her life. A gay ghost stole her boots. And the man who stole her heart stole her memories. Kena plans to get it all back.

Ex-cop Kena's life is filled with regret, beer, and Cheetos. That is, until her ghostly roomie sends her dumpster diving, leading her to a sexy stranger named Luc and a fate she'd rather not remember. As Kena's memories resurface, so do her feelings for Luc, the man she's secretly been in love with for the last thousand years. And he needs her for more than a stroll down memory lane.

Vodou spirits, known as Loa, have been trapped in human form, and are trying to make their way back to the spirit world. But Luc's brother is possessed by a vengeance demon conjured at the hands of NOLA's crime syndicate kingpin. Saving him means damning herself to a spirit prison in a loveless, arranged union with the very man she's supposed to rescue. But not helping Luc's brother sentences him to death, leaving New Orleans in the hands of black magick, and losing Luc forever.

UNBEARABLE

Rose Red will stop at nothing to protect her sister, Snow White, from suffering the same fate as their mother. She vows to kill Hestor, the evil dwarf sorcerer responsible for her death. But a twist of fate lands her on the bottom of a riverbed, and her life in the hands of a mysterious stranger.

Marcus is a beast of a man. He is a bear by day, man by night thanks to a curse from the evil Hestor. But when he meets Rose, he unleashes the real animal. Falling for her is dangerous enough as he must protect the secret of his curse, but she may just be the key to getting his kingdom back.

BAD APPLE

Snow White has always been just that, white as snow. Pure. She's lead a domestic life in the shadow of her outspoken and voluptuous sister, Rose Red. With Rose now marrying Prince Marcus, Snow fears she'll be left with an empty heart and empty cottage.

One night, Snow gives in to her desires. but is caught by Marcus' brother, Prince Darien as he witnesses her indiscretions. But together they tap into a part of Snow long buried, and she's thrown into a world of lust for his flesh.

Once betrayed by Snow's mother, Queen Miriam sees the same thing happening again, this time with her son, Darien. She refuses to let her throne be taken from her a second time, and sets out to kill Snow White. Darien must believe in the power of true love's kiss or lose his kingdom and Snow forever.

ELUDING ILLUSIONS

Emma Banciu dreams about her novels taking on a life of their own. Thanks to a centuries old Gypsy curse, they tend to do just that. Writing with pen and paper she brings things to life, and hell hath no fury like an antagonist scorned. Now she's on the run from Kyrin, an evil demon warlord who surfaced from one of her first manuscripts. And the only way to get rid of him is to destroy the manuscript.

SPECIAL FORCES: OPERATION ALPHA: THE FOX AND THE HOUND KINDLE WORLDS NOVELLA BREAKING THE SEAL BOOK 1

Jayla "Fox" McFadden 'MacGyvered' her way through college and right onto the radar of the CIA. Instead of getting busted, she got offered a job. She's a chemist by day but moonlights on special missions, utilizing her unique talents when needed. She's fought tooth and black-polished nail to make her way in the world and prove she's more than a set of tits.

Noah "Hound" Kendrick is the best tracker on his SEAL team. Haunted by the fact he got his mother killed, he put his body, mind, and soul into the SEALs in retribution, trying to make the world a better place. Nothing gets in the way, especially love, as he refuses to open his heart and lose someone at his expense ever again.

Jayla's teamed with the SEALs for a special assignment. But a squall line from an impending hurricane throws off their plans as Jayla and Noah get separated from the team, washing up on a deserted air force base in the middle of the Pacific Ocean. Now, the Fox and the Hound must survive the elements and each other, as they ride out the physical and emotional storm heading their way.

THE FOX AND THE HOUND 2: KISSES FROM THE KREMLIN COMING MARCH 21ST, 2017.

ABOUT THE AUTHOR:

Wren Michaels hails from the frozen tundra of Wisconsin where beer and cheese are their own food groups. But then a cowboy swept her off her feet and carried her away below the Mason-Dixon line where she promptly lost all tolerance for snow and cold. They decided they'd make beautiful babies together and they got it right on the first try. Now Wren lives happily ever after in the real world and in the worlds of her making, where she creates book boyfriends for the masses to crave.

Find Wren on the Web!

wrenmichaels.com